THE FORGOTTEN COMMANDER

LOST PLANET SERIES: BOOK ONE

USA TODAY BESTSELLING AUTHOR

K WEBSTER

NEW YORK TIMES & USA TODAY BESTSELLING AUTHOR

NICOLE BLANCHARD

CONTENTS

Our planet, Mortuus, is lost and dying.
A desolate place where a few lone survivors dwell.
My men have lost hope. Our future is bleak.
Longevity is a luxury we can't afford.
The most we can hope for is survival.
We've all but given up when an opportunity presents
itself.

Five females—a chance at a future.
Procuring these women went against everything I'd
been taught, but desperate times call for desperate
measures.
They're ours now.
Asleep and made ready for breeding.
We won't die out—lost and forgotten.

It's our destiny to grow and once again inhabit our lonely planet.

I am Breccan Aloisius, the forgotten commander. My people will have the future they deserve. I'll make sure of it.

My mind is made up...until she wakes and nothing goes as planned.

In the beginning, there were many who survived the initial blasts of radiation and the resulting catastrophic environmental disturbances. The morts, the only inhabitants of Mortuus, The Lost Planet, ever changed from the effects of the radiation, learned to adapt and, more importantly, to survive. In doing so, they became highly skilled and intelligent, capable of surviving even the worst conditions.

The planet was dangerous and life wasn't easy, but the morts had each other and that was all that mattered. They flourished in the protective shell of an abandoned building they converted into living quarters. Morts were given jobs, trained from birth in order to pass knowledge from generation to generation.

Eventually, the morts hoped to extend the facility and conquer the wild, untamable outdoors.

Then, disaster struck.

The Rades, a disease contracted from complications of the radiation, began to infect increasing numbers of their population. First, there was fever, followed by sores, then finally madness and, inevitably, death. Quarantining the infected helped, but by then it was too late. Women, children, and the elderly, were the first to go. One by one, morts caught The Rades and died. Whole families wiped away.

Until only ten males remained.

[1]
BRECCAN

Scraaaaaape!

The sound echoes in the command center but it's one I look forward to each solar. Every morning at sunrise, my routine is the same. I slide back the zuta-metal door that hides the massive window that covers the entire wall and allow the sunlight in.

Hot.

Bright.

All-consuming.

I exhale heavily and close my eyes to bask in it. The warmth on my pale white skin heats me to my chilled bones. Ultraviolet rays are harmful to our sensitive flesh but we crave what it offers nonetheless.

"This journey is imperative to our survival," Galen repeats for the millionth time this solar cycle.

I open my eyes just so I can roll them. Gritting my teeth, I drag my gaze from The Graveyard, what we call what's beyond the window, to our faction's botanist. "So you've said," I grunt back, a slight edge to my tone.

Galen frowns and his black irises flicker from round orbs to half-moon slits, a telltale sign of his frustration. Guilt niggles at me for upsetting him. He's only trying to do his job, and he's absolutely correct. But as much as I want to test the soil beyond what we can see of The Graveyard, like he's been suggesting for ages, I'm leery.

"How are the R-levels in the air?" My eyes dart to my closest friend here, Calix.

Calix scratches at his jawline and his pointy ear wiggles on his left side, a common trait when he's deep in thought. His glasses—that once belonged to his father Phalix—sit perched on his head. Phalix perished mysteriously on a trek into The Graveyard. Our best guess was a sabrevipe got him based on the state of his body.

"Hmm," Calix says. His nostrils flare as he taps on his zenotablet and the device lights up in response. After a moment of reading the results, he glances up at me with worry marring his features. "Plus point four."

"Lethal levels are point eight and above," our

2

computer system, Uvie, chirps in her feminine, digitized voice.

Galen lets out a hoot and rises from his chair. If he thinks he's running out there without some sort of plan, he's lost his rekking mind.

"Halt," I bark out. "Plan?"

He puts his large hands on his hips and stares out the window, his onyx orbs gleaming with excitement. The lab coat he always wears over his minnasuit is smeared with soil samples that, if I prayed to any gods, I'd pray have been properly decontaminated. By the way Calix hisses when Galen brushes against his chair, I assume he's just as concerned as I am.

"There," he says, gesturing for the horizon with a sharp black claw. "Beyond Bleex Mountain." He taps the incredibly thick and impenetrable glass, pointing at the highest mountain within our view. Somewhere beyond Bleex Mountain is an old facility that's long been abandoned. "I want to assemble a team and travel there. Five morts. From my calculations, it would only take three full solars to make it there, at least two solars to collect samples, and then three solars back. The data doesn't predict any geostorms anytime soon. Perfect travel conditions." He turns and beams at me, baring the double fangs on each side of his mouth.

"No." My instant reaction is always no. It's unsafe.

Despite the R-levels being in the mild zone, there are other threats. Sabrevipes are known to prowl the area, especially in good weather. They're rekking huge, vicious, and tricky to kill. At least their meat is worth eating.

"We could always expand our search beyond the old Sector 1779 to see if maybe we find any working facilities—"

I cut Galen off with a warning growl. He presents this argument often, and even Calix agrees that it's a terrible idea to go traipsing across The Graveyard in hopes of finding any mort life or working facilities.

"Breccan," Galen says in a low voice. "We have to try. What if the soil is good for planting? We could take the seedlings that aren't thriving and replant them."

I wave a hand at him to dismiss his words. "The seedlings will die." We'll *all* die.

He flinches as though I've struck him. "But we need this for our survival because eventually—"

"No!" I roar, fisting my hands as I storm over to the window. I stare out into the barren wasteland outside of our mountain home and shake my nog. It's dead. A few animals roam about that are worth capturing and eating, but other than that, it's worthless space. Empty. Desolate. Rekking cruel. Rage bubbles up inside my chest and my ears flatten against my nog, a natural mort physiological reaction when preparing for a fight. "What good are thriving seedlings when our own race is dying out? The thing we need for the continuity of our people are females. And as you can see," I hiss and gesture to the empty nothingness, "there isn't anyone left."

The room goes quiet aside from Calix's tapping on his zenotablet. Galen and I get into this argument often and it's in everyone's best interest to stay out of the middle. It's come to blows before, and I'm still nursing bruised ribs from the last time Galen got angry when I told him no. He's mostly calm but loses himself to bouts of rage. Avrell, our doctor, has explained to me numerous times that it's a chemical reaction because of his genetics and not an innate desire to drive me out of my mortarekking mind.

"Why don't we just invite a sabrevipe into our facility?" Galen bites back, his fury rearing its ugly nog. "Why don't we let it tear us to shreds and suck on our bones because we have no rekking future?!"

My own anger is snuffed as guilt once again takes its place.

He's right.

Again.

"Galen—"

My apology is cut short when a trumpeting blare goes off. All discussions are ignored as the three of us take off at a sprint to the ship deck.

Theron and Sayer are back.

And the blare means good news.

Our boots slap the floors, echoing in the empty corridors as we run. When we reach the thick, double-reinforced door, each of us fumbles to quickly pull on our zu-gear. The thick material will protect us from mild to medium R-levels and our masks will keep out any airborne pathogens that could be harmful to our health.

Within seconds, we're dressed and protected, each of us eager for a tiny morsel of good news. I key in the sixteen-digit code that only a few of us have and then we push through the heavy door.

Theron and Sayer, fully decked out in their own zu-gear, are already jumping from the ship and running our way.

"What did you find?"

"Were there any signs of life?"

"Did you scavenge anything we can use?"

Calix, Galen, and I all blurt out our questions at once. Theron raises his hand to silence us.

"Commander," Theron says, grinning through the

glass of his mask. "You're going to lose your rekking mind."

Sayer nods rapidly beside him. Their excitement is palpable. It can only mean good things for the faction.

"It's something you need to see to believe," Sayer tells me and starts for the ship.

We storm after them and up the ramp into the vessel.

Upon entering, I see the cargo area filled with what looks like cryotubes. Five, to be exact. They're certainly not anything from Mortuus but I do remember reading about them in the library of books left behind by those who've encountered them before us. The same books that taught us everything from mechanics and technology to reproduction and biology, but not this. This is unchartered territory.

"What's in them?" I demand.

Theron raps a gloved knuckle on the top of one. "Look."

I stalk over to him and peer into the small window —and find myself staring at the strangest creature I've ever laid eyes on.

Lips similar to mine but much plumper and an odd shade of pink are the first thing I notice. The nose on the alien is pert and adorned with a device that looks to be used for breathing. Light brown markings speckle her flesh. Long, dark lashes fan the creature's high cheekbones and an obscene amount of brown hair— the same color as my favorite root tea—frames her face.

Her.

Her.

Her.

Images from *those* books—books meant for older, mating morts—are forefront in my mind. Books that explained in detail not only mort anatomy, but also how two morts physically fit together to reproduce. The same books that every rekking mort in this facility has memorized and looked at for their own selfish reasons. Books we never imagined we'd get to use what we'd learned.

But now?

"W-What is this?" I drag my gaze to Theron. "Where did you get this creature?"

His grin is cold. "We were orbiting our planet in the *Mayvina* just outside the atmosphere, sending out pings. You know, the usual, searching for life."

"And we pinged something huge. A cruiser," Sayer explains, also grinning. His double fangs glisten in the light.

"A cruiser?" I growl. "What did you do?"

Theron shrugs and gestures to the cryotubes. "We detected life on the vessel. Hundreds. However, they had some life protected in these units, as though they were put in stasis for some reason. Being the slick mortarekkers we are, Sayer and I boarded the ship, slipped as many cryotubes into the *Mayvina* as would fit, before the vessel went into hyperspeed and disappeared. I'm telling you, it was a chance. A small sliver, and we took it. These are ours."

I stare into the window again, mesmerized by the intriguing creature. "Have Avrell ready the lab. I want all steps being taken to ensure we don't expose the facility to disease. Only open this one pod but keep the alien in stasis. I want Avrell to test her biological code."

Four pairs of intense stares are on me. The hope is bright in their onyx eyes. Guys who never smile are grinning like it's their rekking job. Something fills my chest.

Hope.

"And if they're a match?" Galen asks lowly, his voice slightly muffled behind his protective mask.

"If they're a match, we breed."

NINE MORTS STAND all too close to Avrell as he works quickly to study the biological data. It's been six solars since Theron and Sayer brought home the cryotubes and we've all been on edge with the need to know if breeding will work. Galen's seedling mission is a thing of the past. Nobody wants to leave the lab, much less the facility, to trek through The Graveyard hunting for good soil to plant.

"There are only five of them," mutters Hadrian, the youngest mort at only seventeen revolutions old. "Who will get one?"

I drag my gaze from the unconscious alien who remains in a deep sleep to the only mortling in our faction. Memories of when his mother died, the last of our females, is a dark solar I try desperately not to remember. Vetta was like a mother to all of us. And because she was still fertile, we had plans to keep our existence going via her womb. That all faded away the solar she caught The Rades and died shivering while she clawed at her own flesh, lost to the madness of the disease.

The child in her womb, one that belonged to her deceased mate Puno, passed along with her. It was a devastating moment. I took Hadrian under my protection and have looked after him as a son ever since.

"Yeah, Commander, who will get one?" Draven, our faction's lieutenant engineer, challenges from the doorway of the lab. I know he won't step inside. He suffers mentally and always feels trapped. It all stems, according to Avrell and his studies, from when Draven caught a mild case of The Rades. He was in a sleeplike state for almost an entire revolution—hundreds and hundreds of solars. His skin seeped with a puss-like substance from sores that had formed all over his body. If it hadn't been for Avrell caring for him at every moment of every solar, he would have met death along with Vetta and her unborn mortling. When he came to, his eyes were crazed and he babbled on for many solar cycles about "the captors." They'd chained him up and tortured him.

All in his mind, of course.

They still haunt him with every breath he takes.

It's been many revolutions, and he's never lost the unhinged glimmer in his coal-black eyes.

I straighten my spine and walk over to the alien. Avrell has taken to calling her Specimen Az-1. Her chest, beneath the thin sheet covering, rises and falls with each breath she takes. We're all wearing our zu-gear until we can ascertain if she's carrying anything harmful.

"Any updates?" I ask, my eyes glued to her unusual, dirty-looking face. She has skin the color of a sabrevipe's belly. If she weren't potentially dangerous to touch, I'd love to remove my glove and see what the texture of her flesh feels like.

He looks up from the micro-viewer on the table near the alien, and a small smile, revealing his semi-filed-down fangs, has hope once again dancing inside my chest. "I think it's good news, Commander."

Everyone in the room seems to be holding their breath. The tension is thick enough to cut with a magknife.

"Proceed," I urge, tamping down my eagerness.

"Have a look." He gestures to the micro-viewer.

I walk over to the machine and peer into the viewer. Inside are colorful cells but they mean nothing to me.

"See the cerulean cells?" he asks.

"There are many," I agree.

"Now find the opaque ones. You may have to squint to see those."

I blink as I attempt to focus. "I see them. The cerulean ones are being eaten by them."

"Not eaten," Avrell says, a smile in his voice. "Fertilized."

I jerk away and glare at him. "What does it mean?"

"Exactly what you think. Not only is our genetics compatible, but we can breed the aliens. That right there," he gestures to the micro-viewer, "is the hope for our survival."

"What will you do with them?" There were at least four fertilized cell units under the viewer.

"I could destroy them or I could implant them."

I look around to the other eight pair of eyes watching my exchange with Avrell. Ten morts. Five aliens. It's unfair to choose between who gets an alien to mate with and who doesn't. As much as I'd love to wake and mate with them properly, it's too risky. If the aliens were to fall ill and pass on like Vetta, all of this would be for nothing.

My ears flatten against my nog as I crack all twenty-eight of the sub-bones in my neck. All my subordinates slightly bow their nogs in submission. They know my word is binding. Even if they'll hate what I'm about to say.

"Keep them in stasis," I say, despising my own words. "Gather samples from all ten of us and implant the fertilized cells into all of their wombs. Keep any extra samples frozen for future use in case these don't take. This is the only hope for our future at this time."

My morts all wear the same tortured expressions that I'm sure I do.

We want them.

We want them awake and we want to mate with them. *Need* to mate with them. Not only as a biological imperative to ensure our survival, but to remind us of what it means to *live* instead of merely survive.

But sacrifice is in our blood. It's all we've done our entire lives. The sacrifice will end with us, though. These implanted cells will grow into mortlings. Mortlings will grow into doctors and leaders and fighters. Families will be bred from our sacrifices. One solar soon, this facility will bustle with life and activity. Our sacrifices will be worth it.

At least that's what I'll keep telling myself.

"I'll be in the command center," I mutter before excusing myself.

An addictive dose of ultraviolet rays is much needed because I'd do just about anything to bring a little light to my nearly pitch-black future.

Sacrifice.

It must be done.

[2]
ARIA

I'M DROWNING.

Waves of pain suck me under, pulling at my limbs, making them heavy and hard to operate. An invisible weight crushes my chest and I fight to draw oxygen into my protesting lungs. *Too much.* I did too much flora the night before. A newer drug to the market that's more accepted among high society. No needles or smoking for the rich and famous. Just a quick inhalation of the expensive mist and you're lost to it. Its seductive call sings to me, tempting me to go back under and escape.

That's why I became an actress in the first place. I wanted to go somewhere else, be someone else. I had the body, the face, the talent. The money was a factor, but it was only the vehicle that gave me access to my true goal: escape. Getting out of the slums, out of my life. Fame and fortune bought me a way out, but it never truly brought me happiness like I'd imagined.

Too late, I'd realized I'd been seduced by the very glitz and glamour I'd been groomed to emulate. There was no escape, there was only another cage—albeit a gilded one.

The rolling tide of drugs both soothes and torments. I alternate between the highest I've ever been and the most pain I've ever experienced. The latter slams into my body like an unforgiving tide, over and over, never ending. I try, uselessly, to open my eyes, to press the buttons on the controls to deliver another dose to end the pain, or rip out the needle supplying it, but I can do neither. The very thing that has given me my only release is now my greatest torment.

Minutes, hours, days, I can't even tell how much time passes before I'm able to move my hands—and then it's only to open and close my fingers. I can't move my arms from my sides. By sheer force of will, I crack my eyelids open and wince at the too-bright room surrounding me.

I try not to panic. It isn't the first time I've found myself in a strange home after a long night of dancing and drinking and it won't be the last. But I'd never taken it so far that I couldn't remember how I'd gotten there. That I couldn't even move the next morning.

You've done it this time, Aria.

But it's the next wave of pain that brings me fully awake, driving away the last remnants of stupor and spawning the first flash of fear. Cramps steal across my stomach and drive downward. My body trying to purge itself. I've been hungover before, but nothing like this. Nothing that makes me feel like I'm dying.

Another scream rips from my throat and draws the attention of the guard on the other side of the door. Only I must still be dreaming, because the man who comes through looks like something from a nightmare, all eerie white skin and misshapen bones on his forehead. He towers by my bedside in a strange suit, with flowing black hair and hard, black eyes that glare at me from underneath a heavy brow. Fangs. He has fangs. Definitely not human. A monster.

This is a nightmare.

Not real.

The image of him swims as the pain intensifies. My mouth waters and I can feel bile rise in the back of my throat. Panic assails me when I try to wrench my hands up to cover my mouth but they're restrained.

Restrained, in pain, at the mercy of a monster in a

room I don't recognize. How could this morning get any worse?

Then the door opens, and nine more giants in varying degrees of terrifying step into the room.

Unwilling or unable to keep my eyes open and face this horror, I'll never know which, I give in to the riptides of pain and shock pulling me under and succumb to the welcoming darkness.

THE NEXT TIME I WAKE, clear-headed with a hollow feeling in my stomach, it's to an empty room, the door unguarded.

Maybe it had been a nightmare after all. It had to be. I must have overdosed again and they'd taken me to an exclusive healing resort to clean out my system. In a week or two, they'll ship me back to Hollywood, dope me up to get through another week of rehearsals, appearances, and tapings, and then repeat.

Except...this resort is nothing like any of the others they've ever stuck me in. They may treat me like a trained animal for their amusement, but even so, I'm a *spoiled* pet. In return for good behavior and press, I receive the best care, food, transportation and lodging.

At one point, it must have been a nice place, the

crème de la crème of technological advances. There are screens embedded into the walls that read out my vitals from sensors attached to my wrists, chest, and temples. Except, the technology is years out of date, usable, but clunky and sluggish. The room is clean and well-maintained, but the white walls have faded with time and cracks spider-web across the surface.

It doesn't matter. I'll just call my assistant and have them pick me up early. I have a show in two days and we start shooting two days after that, I think. Actually, I'm not sure. Everything's so hazy in my mind. I don't even know what day or time it is or where the hell I'm at, but there's no way I can take any time off now. I'm never able to take vacations so I certainly don't have time for a rehab stint. They must know that. I need to get ahold of Kevin. As my talent manager, he'll help me make sense of all this.

I climb out of the bed and scurry over to one of the computer screens, despite the soreness in my stomach that must have come from them pumping the drugs from my system, and frown. The dark green backdrop and flashing readouts don't look like any other operating system I've ever used. Maybe it's some sort of retro deal? I press menu options randomly, hoping to find a familiar command, to no avail.

What in the hell place have they stuck me in?

The aching in my stomach increases and I remember the dream. The waves of pain. It should scare me how much I've let the drugs take over my life, but there are worse things than risking my health to cope with my choices.

I block out the soreness as I move to a different screen. This one sets off an alarm the moment I touch it and I whirl around in surprise, my body screaming in protest. Wetness floods my panties and for the first time in a long time, I feel the stirrings of embarrassment. Have I really fallen so far that I can't even control my bodily functions?

As the alarms blare in the background, I stumble around the room and search for the bathroom. There's no way in hell I'll let anyone see me in this state. They may require confidentiality at places like this, but gossip is a hot commodity and everyone can be bought if the price is right. I'm living proof of that.

I find the bathroom on the second try. The first door contained a supply closet with more outdated technology, including odd breathing masks, tablet screens and handheld devices. I don't even want to know what the bodysuits are for.

A shower will help clear my mind. Then everything will start making sense.

I waste ten minutes trying to figure out the controls

for the odd shower stall until I give up. When the attendants come back, I'll have them show me how to use it. Until then, I'll just change out of my dirty clothes and hope I don't smell. I strip from the hospital gown and throw it in a corner.

I almost do the same with my serviceable underwear—then I spot the blood.

My vision swims and my ears ring so loudly, I can no longer hear the alarm. I force myself to discard the panties along with the hospital gown. Then I give myself instructions. First step, use the washcloth on the lip of the sink to wash as best you can. *Find the soap, Aria. Wash your body, Aria.* Don't imagine what horrors caused the blood. Don't think. That's the number one rule. Don't think. Just do.

Act like reality is the lie and fantasy is the truth.

I don't know how long I stand in front of the mirror once I've done a cursory washing. Too long. Not long enough. The alarms blare until I can't hear my own thoughts—which is probably a good thing.

When they shut off, I know I'm no longer alone. The silence is deafening, palpable. I thought I couldn't be more ashamed of the situations I put myself in, but I was wrong. This must be a new low.

I brace myself for their judgement as I hear voices on the other side of the bathroom door. They'll whisper behind their hands. Give me pitying glances. It won't be long before my latest stunt winds up on every tabloid from sea to shining sea, but I won't let them break me. I'll face them, then my talent manager, and I'll be Aria Delaney, the A-list actress and party girl they want me to be. And I'll do it with a smile.

The door opens and I take one last moment to breathe before I finish my ablutions. I locate another paper gown in a cabinet to dress in and pray blood won't continue to drip down my legs. With sluggish movements, I put the gown on and then step toward the door and turn to face my fate.

Instead of the nurses I'm expecting, I find the men from my nightmares.

All ten of them squeeze into the tiny hospital room and try to wedge themselves in the doorway. Their big, broad shoulders don't quite fit, and three of them get stuck in the door. It would be comical if it weren't so terrifying.

I knot my hands together, between my breasts, and blink. Flora isn't normally hallucinogenic, but sometimes it comes laced with other drugs with varying side effects. That's all.

"Help," I croak to anyone but the monsters crowding my way.

They all snap their eyes to mine the moment I speak.

"Step back," comes a commanding, oddly accented voice. "Let Avrell have room or I'll throw every rekking one of you out into The Graveyard."

Rekking?

The Graveyard?

What is this madness?

The three in the doorway move back obediently, but their eyes strain to see me around two more who take a step forward. One of whom is clearly in charge —the one who'd leaned over my bedside when I'd woken up before. There's no way I'd ever forget his face. Not only because it was so odd, but because he'd looked at me with such contempt.

The other by his side bears no such expression, and I immediately prefer his presence.

"Hello," the kind one says. "My name is Avrell Dracarion. Do you understand my language?"

"Yes," I croak. "How?"

One of the other aliens waves at me and smiles, baring not one but two upper fangs on each side of his mouth. Like a double dose of vampire. Twice as many deadly teeth. "The name's Sayer, linguistics specialist," he says, his grin growing wider. I'm sure he thinks he's being friendly but I can't stop staring at his teeth that

look way too sharp for my comfort. "You can understand us because Uvie and I have worked for years on
inputting all neighboring planetary languages into the
mainframe. Right, Uvie?"

A computerized woman speaks. "Correct. Each
mort has been implanted with a specially designed
language interpretation unit that allows them to speak
and understand languages that have been input into
the system. The moment you spoke, it enacted their
interpretation units. Their brains work behind the
scenes to do all the computing, so that it comes natu-
rally for the morts. Some words, however, won't trans-
late due to interplanetary slangs that may have formed
since the last update to the language mainframe."

Speaking of brains, mine hurts. I'm dreaming. This
is all in my head. But they all stare at me in an expec-
tant way. Vivid and real. They're not going away.

I lick my lips as I glance back and forth between
them. "What's going on?"

The two before me share a look, then the one
called Avrell says, "Please, don't be frightened."

"I'm way the hell past frightened." It was a miracle
my knees didn't simply give out right from under me.
"You...I don't even know what you are. I don't know
what's happening. I just want to go home, please."

"We aren't going to hurt you." Avrell holds up his

hands. Large, pale white hands with bony, oddly protruding knuckles. What's most frightening though are the half-inch black claws on the tips of each of his fingers. Sharp and brutal. Something that would belong to a wild animal. Claws that look like they could peel my flesh right from my bones. My heart pounds quicker in my chest. "We aren't going to hurt you," he repeats and takes a slow step forward. I inch back in response.

The tall one next to Avrell sighs as if annoyed and crosses his arms over his chest.

"Who are all of you? *What* are you?"

"I am a healer." He places a hand on the shoulder of the giant next to him. "This is Breccan Aloisius, the chief commander of the facility. This is our planet, Mortuus."

"Is she healthy or isn't she, Av?" one of them asks from the hospital room beyond.

There is a murmuring of agreement from the group.

The giant barks out what must be a command to the group, and the men file out of the room while shooting me curious looks.

"Please, tell me what's going on."

The giant steps forward. "We've brought you to our planet because we are the last of our race." He glances down at my feet and then up along my thighs. His mouth twists. "It doesn't seem as though you will be of any help. Your implantation was unsuccessful."

I follow his gaze and find my inner thighs coated with blood. "Implantation?"

Then it dawns on me.

I've been kidnapped—and it wasn't an assault or menstrual cycle that caused my bleeding. These... whatever they are, have kidnapped me and tried to get me pregnant. The blood is from a miscarriage.

[3]
BRECCAN

I'M SO REKKING ANGRY, I could destroy the entire lab with only my two fists. I would, too, if I were alone. Each morsel of hope we're given, gets devoured by some unseen force. Perhaps our destiny isn't to grow and repopulate Mortuus. Perhaps we are meant to die. My hand shakes with fury and I have the overwhelming urge to go to the command center and calm myself with some ultraviolet therapy. Unknown to Avrell, it helps more than it hurts. He'd put me in a reform cell though if he knew how much *therapy* I self-administered each day.

It's been six solar cycles—a total of forty-two solars—since Avrell collected her eggs and fertilized them with the samples from all the morts. He implanted one of the fertilized eggs and it seemed to have been thriving.

Until she woke up.

"Put her back in cryosleep and—"

"W-What?" she hisses, stumbling backward, her blood dripping all over the sterile floor. Even with Avrell's constant reassurance that she's safe and uncontaminated, I still worry over infectious diseases being spread among my crew.

Ignoring her, I pierce Avrell with a stern glare. "Cryosleep. Now. Specimen Az-1 is incompatible. Start on the next specimen."

"I have a name!" she yells, her voice echoing off the stark walls around me.

She hugs her middle and shivers. Silent tears roll down her speckled cheeks and drip from her jaw, soaking the front of her paper gown. A pang of sympathy tugs at my heart but I can't allow myself to grow soft over a useless alien woman. We have to keep trying.

"After I treat her womb with some microbots to heal the area, we could attempt implantation again almost immediately," Avrell offers, his dark eyebrows pinched together.

Microbots can heal just about anything. Loss of limbs though, you're simply out of luck. His pitch-black hair—which matches in color with every male in this facility—is messy this solar. As though he's been yanking at it. Unlike my long locks that hang loosely down my back, he keeps his hair clipped short—says it interferes with his work. The toll his studies are taking on his physical form is evident. Every mort in this facility is at his breaking point.

"I don't think we should lose hope yet," he says softly. "Specimen Az-1's body seems to be purging out some toxins that were lying dormant while in cryosleep. Foreign toxins."

"I'm Aria," she whispers. "And it's called flora. I was high on flora."

Aria.

The name sounds like a song. Thoughts of my mother's voice humming sweet words claw at me from the inside. I refuse to remember that fateful solar when I stared into her sad eyes as blood ran from the corners, stealing her from me.

"Please," she begs.

The blood pools on the floor between her feet and I cringe. Disgusting. What a mess. "I'm sorry but—"

Avrell cuts me off. "The embryo was yours, Commander."

A confusing mixture of pride and grief settles in

my bones. The mortling that was growing inside of Specimen Az-1—*Aria*—belonged to me.

Perhaps it is I who am broken.

"I can test one of the other morts next," Avrell utters, his thoughts one with my own.

"Hell no!" Aria screeches, causing my ears to flatten against my nog to block out the sound.

Irritation bubbles up inside of me. I'm used to my men obeying my commands. This Aria is difficult.

"It's for your own good," I growl.

Her brown eyes that match her tea-colored hair flare with fury. Her cheeks beneath the speckles burns bright red. I expect more argument from the problematic alien. But one quick glance to the door behind me is my only warning that she's no longer interested in talking.

With surprising speed, she darts for the doorway, slipping only slightly in her pool of blood.

On instinct, I reach out to grab her. My claws swipe the air, raking across her paper gown, and tear gashes along the side of it but don't make purchase.

"Halt!" I bellow, jerking out of my stupor as I charge after her.

Bloody red footprints are left in her wake as she pushes through the door and runs down the corridor.

"Lock her in," I yell to Avrell as I chase down my disruptive alien.

She's much faster than I could ever have imagined but I train every solar to be faster than sabrevipes. I pick up my speed and race after her. An alarm sounds and then the hiss of doors automatically closing tells me Avrell's done his job. Soon, she'll have nowhere to go and I'll have her in my grip.

I pass by several doors where curious black eyes peer through the glass. They'll soon learn all about our little runaway.

I have to catch her first.

She slows when she realizes she's running straight for a dead end. Her nog darts to the left and then to the right before she lets out a terrified shriek. Wide brown eyes meet mine as she turns to face me. I slow to a trot, now that I have her trapped. Her gaze travels behind me. If she thinks she's going to make it past me, she's lost her rekking mind.

"It's in your best interest to comply," I say calmly.

Her nostrils flare and her eyes become watery. "I don't want to go back to sleep." She bites down on one of her swollen pink lips. "If you don't plan on letting me go home, can't you just let me hang out with you?"

I blink at her, confused by her words, momentarily

stunned by her vulnerability. After a second, I shake my nog to clear it. "No."

She holds out both of her tiny palms as if she has the power to stop my massive frame. Small and delicate. Shaky. A bluish tint shades her slender fingers. Her teeth begin to clack together and I cock my nog to the side, curious at the sounds she's making. When the sounds become louder, I worry she's about to strike.

I straighten my spine, letting my sub-bones crack and pop as I rise to my full height. My ears flatten against my nog and I bare my double fangs at her. Whatever battle move she's about to unleash, I'll be ready. I've taken on sabrevipes with my bare hands. I can take down this miniature alien.

But instead of attacking me, she cowers, a terrified sob escaping her.

I frown at her, breaking my battle stance. "I can see you're afraid," I start, choosing my words carefully. She reminds me of so many of our people...*from before.* When they were all screaming and begging for their lives as The Rades wiped them out one by one. I squeeze my eyes shut, overwhelmed by the reminder.

Slap! Slap! Slap!

I blink my eyes open just in time to see her attempting to dart past me, her bare feet slapping the tile.

Lightning quick, I strike out and tangle my fist in her hair before she can get too far. A bone-rattling scream rips from her tiny body. She wiggles and squirms. Her claws, softer and more brittle than mine, rake across my cheek as she tries to free herself. She doesn't break the surface but the sting remains. I grab her by her tiny arms and push her against the nearest door. Draven's wild eyes watch the show from beyond the glass. When I glower at him, he disappears from my sight.

"Halt," I order, my chest heaving from exertion.

Her throat bobs as she swallows. "Just kill me," she says, her voice wobbling. "I'd rather be dead than be trapped in some coffin."

I cock my nog to the side and study her lips. Once, Jareth ate a new species of flatshrooms Galen discovered and had a violent reaction. His lips swelled up like this untamed one's. But his were never so intriguing. We jested at his expense until Avrell administered a treatment to heal him.

But these lips?

These are a visual snare, and I am caught.

She licks them.

Heat, fast like the flash of a magnastrike in a geostorm, strikes my lower belly. Like ultraviolet poisoning entering my bloodstream when I've spent one too many solars stealing extra seconds in the sun, it awakens my nerves as it travels to my cock. So many times I've stroked myself to release just to find a tiny inkling of pleasure in my bleak world. So many times.

And now, dark, forbidden thoughts of pleasuring myself in other ways begin to take root inside my mind.

As if sensing my physiological reaction to her, Aria licks her lips again. Her lids grow heavy and she gives me a sweet smile. A smile I want to taste.

A low rumbling builds in my throat.

Possessive and animalistic.

Mine.

The thought is like when Hadrian used to spill his cups as a small mortling. Fast. Out of control. Messy. You can't stop it once it starts. Images of Aria free of her paper gown and spread before me are on the forefront of my mind. My cock is rigid in my minnasuit, straining against the protective material.

We could breed the natural way.

Like my parents and their parents and every mort before them.

Perhaps being in cryosleep *was* the problem. Avrell may have been onto something when he'd mentioned the foreign toxins hiding. I could claim this little alien as mine and shoot my seed into her over and over again until it finally rekking sticks.

An infant.

Mine.

Birth to a new hope.

"Please," she begs, fresh new tears streaking down her odd-looking face.

The animal in me craves to flit out my forked tongue and lap up her wetness. So feral and untamed. I've had her in my arms for mere seconds and she's already making me forget who I am.

Is she infecting me?

Am I losing my mind like Draven did when he caught The Rades?

Did Avrell miss an important detail?

Before I can consider those thoughts, her eyelashes flutter as her eyes roll back, and then her knees buckle. I pull her into my arms. Her body is light and soft. It's her scent though that makes its way into my nostrils and lays claim to my lungs.

Sweet.

Foreign.

Mine.

I breathe her in but don't let her out.

Running my clawed finger through her silky hair, I become enraptured by her softness. My mind runs with ideas of where else she could be soft. I'm still rock hard in my suit and eager to learn more about her.

She's so small and fragile looking as she sleeps. Her plump lips taunt me as she parts them in slumber. I wonder what they taste like. My cock throbs against my thigh and seeps with need. The smart thing to do would be to march back to the lab and toss her back into the pod. I've always done what needs to be done for the betterment of our people.

So how come I'm walking down the corridor past all the curious eyes and bypassing the lab?

The plans have changed, that's why.

Little alien Aria belongs to me.

And I'm going to put my mortarekking seed inside of her.

"GREETINGS, COMMANDER," Uvie greets me as I enter the command center.

"Sleep mode," I instruct, not wanting even the computer to be a witness to my overwhelming needs. My body is shaking. Withdrawals.

Earlier, instead of running off with her like I'd originally planned, I'd reluctantly turned around and took Aria back to the lab to have Avrell clean her up while I handle some necessary business.

My mind is racing.

I'm losing control.

Which is why I need to get ahold of myself.

Closing the door behind me, I stride into the empty command center over to the thick zuta-metal door that covers the window. It makes a loud racket as I drag it open, inviting the sun's harmful rays into the room.

As soon as the heat hits my flesh, my veins feel as though they're tingling with pleasure. I unzip the front of my minnasuit and tug the material down and off my arms. It hangs at my waist, the arms swinging around at my sides. Dark red clouds brew in the distance and I can tell the winds are high this solar based on all the debris blowing past. A geostorm is headed our way and it appears to be massive.

The sun's rays soak into my skin, heating my flesh to unsafe levels. Ever since the solar when we were forced from our once livable planet into the safety of the mountain facility to escape The Rades, our flesh is incredibly vulnerable to UV rays. Avrell thinks we all caught a case of it, albeit minor, and this is what caused the change. Not only will the rays produce painful, infection-causing burns, but we can also grow intoxicated by the rays' poisoning. Too much is lethal.

But a little...

Dizziness washes over me, chasing away my

responsibilities and worry. I fall into a chair near the window and tilt my nog back, exposing my neck to the sun. My chest aches as the heated rays penetrate me. But the buzzing running through my veins makes it worth it. Whispers dance inside my nog. Flutters skim across my throat and then along my torso. My cock jolts in my suit, reminding me it needs attention.

With a groan, I slide my large hand beneath the fabric and seek out my erection. It's hard and aching. My seed already weeping from the tip. I crave to hunt down alien Aria and pin her down. To mount her, push my cock inside her, and rut against her until I'm spent and sated. Our future taking root inside her. Imagining her nakedness below me as whimpers of pleasure escape in her sweet voice, I find myself stroking my thickness.

"Let me help you."

Her voice is a purr.

A hallucination.

Figments of the intoxicating UV poison running rampant in my system.

"Aria," I growl, her name a worshipful word on my forked tongue.

I'm rutting and rutting.

Driving deep into her warm body.

Releasing our future into her womb.

"Rekk!" I hiss, the pleasure exploding through me.

Heat shoots up and splatters my singed abdomen that is already beginning to bubble up with sores. I need to close the window but I'm still blissed out on the poison.

No worries.

No fear.

No loss of hope.

Just pure, unfiltered pleasure.

A rattling outside the door jerks me from my stupor. I stand on shaky legs and barely manage to get my suit pulled back on when the door swings open.

Avrell has a protective arm around Aria. His brows are furrowed as he assesses the situation. He's had to drag me out of here in worse states, many times before. This need I have isn't anything new.

"Here," he says as he tugs a cloth from his pocket and tosses it my way.

I clean off my chest and then tug the zipper up, hiding my scorched flesh that no longer is soaked with my seed. I shove the soiled cloth into my pocket and try not to sway on my feet.

"How long have you been in here?" Avrell asks. With a small sigh, he stalks by to drag the big zuta-metal door closed.

Uvie, the piece of rogshite computer, chirps, ratting me out. "Eight minutes and forty-six seconds."

"Someone doesn't understand sleep mode," I gripe. "How is she?" I tip my nog to Aria, who watches me with a glint of fear in her stare. So unlike the expression she wore in my fantasy. My cock thickens once more. Is this how it will be now? The need to breed with her dictating my every thought and action?

Little alien Aria is my new poison.

"I've checked her over. Her body is done purging the unsuccessful implantation and the microbots have healed the area. She is physically ready to try again." He glances over at her, concern written all over his face. Then he regards me with a look of resignation. "Are you sure about this?"

When I'd brought her unconscious form to the lab earlier, I told him of the new plan. Aria will be the vessel of our future. Avrell can continue to impregnate the aliens in cryosleep, but Aria is mine to test in real time. She will sleep in my quarters. She will answer to me. She will bear my young.

This. Will. Work.

"Absolutely," I say with fierce conviction.

He bows his nog in submission.

It begins now.

[4]
ARIA

THIS MONSTER ALIEN, or whatever they are, wants me to have his baby.

I can't quite wrap my mind around the one I lost, let alone the prospect of having to go through the process to make another, especially not with him. Having a family, children had never been in my plan. It couldn't be, not with my lifestyle. Not only would it be impossible to take care of a family with my schedule, but my body was my number one commodity. Having a baby would ruin me.

But breeding with the alien may be my only shot at survival in this strange world and I'm nothing if not a master of survival.

The commander, who I understand will be the one I'm staying with, takes my arm and practically drags me down the long, winding hallways of the facility. I try to memorize the route we take from the room we found him in, but after one too many turns, I lose the map in my head. Panic threatens to overtake me, but I tamp it down. Desperation leads to mistakes, and I can't afford to make any mistakes if I'm going to make it home alive.

As the sea of doors fly past, I attempt to look in them to see how many others I'm dealing with, but most, if not all, are empty. It's in line with what I've gathered from the doctor, Avrell, and their desire to breed with any available women. Occasionally, one of the windows will reveal a blurred face like the commander's. The strange pale skin, intimidating stature and dark, thick hair.

But no women.

It should scare me more than it does. At first, I *was* terrified. But once I realized they were relying on me, that there was something I could use to bargain with, the fear faded away and was replaced by resolve. I've done worse things and survived. I can do this, too.

I'll spread my legs for this alien as long as it keeps me alive.

Finally, the commander stops at one of the doors and lifts his wrist bracelet to the scanner. A beep sounds and the door slides open to reveal what must be his quarters. He grunts and tugs at my arm, pulling me inside behind him.

He leaves me in the entryway of his quarters to shed his uniform in an alcove that I assume is the bathroom. I'm grateful. Much as he terrifies me, it also didn't escape my notice what he'd been doing when the doctor and I interrupted him. There was no denying the scent that still clung heavy in the air, or the slack, well-pleasured ease to his muscles.

Had I done that?

The concept is hard to forget as I watch him strip out of his uniform and toss it into a hole in the wall that I assume is a laundry chute. Beneath is a thin, skin-tight under-layer of some sort that forms to the well-defined ridges of his bulging muscles. I wrap my arms around my waist, but I can't tear my eyes away.

"You may wear my clothes. Open the cubicle there," he instructs, and nods to a wall of cabinets opposite the bed.

Ignoring the bed, and its implications, I peer into the cabinets. I grab clothes at random until I find a pair of pants with a sort-of elastic waist and a shirt that's nearly a dress. I take as long as possible, hoping to find him already in bed. Surely after rubbing one out, he can't possibly be ready for another round.

"Why did you steal me?" I croak out.

He lets out a heavy sigh. "We didn't steal you. We found you. My men were doing a run and located some life in a passing vessel. They pulled them from the vessel and brought them back here."

That makes no sense, though.

Why would I be sleeping in some pod creeping through outer space?

"Turn around," he says, and his voice comes closer behind than I expect.

As much as I'd hoped I'd be given a night of reprieve, evidence suggests Commander Breccan is eager to apply himself to the task.

Throat dry, hands trembling, I pivot to face him and my fate. No amount of deep breathing or calming techniques will soothe my nerves, but there is one trick I've learned through my years of acting—both in front of the camera and off. Faking it. It's what I do. The only thing I know how to do.

I wish I had a hit of flora. Their system—though out of date—is still very advanced and managed to clean my whole body of every trace of the drug. They need their perfect breeder, after all, so I don't even have detoxing to distract me from the way he's looking at me.

"Maybe we should get some sleep," I suggest. "It's been a long day." I start to move in the direction of the bed, but he stops me with a grunt and I freeze before turning back to face him, dread pooling in my stomach.

He's so close, his body blots out everything else. Wide shoulders, thickly muscled abdomen, narrow hips framing his sex. I use my own inspection to distract me from the feeling of his eyes tracing my body. I'm acutely aware of the fact that despite the clothes he's provided me, there was no underwear. His flat nose flares and I wonder if his senses are so strong that he can smell my fear, because it certainly won't be arousal at this point.

"We won't be sleeping. Avrell informed me you will be fertile for the next week. We can't afford to miss any chance to reproduce."

"How romantic," I mumble.

His gaze catches mine. "Romance has nothing to do with reproduction." He says it almost like a question.

There's a pause, where I can either panic or submit to this hand I've been dealt. I know I have no chance of fighting these men. They're bigger, stronger, and more knowledgeable about the terrain. Frustration builds inside me like a geyser and no doubt shoots from my eyes to his. I hate him, in this moment, for putting me in this position. I hate him for taking my choices away, like so many others.

But I won't let him win.

I won't be a victim.

I'm not sure how I ended up in that cryotube in the first place, but it landed me on this planet and now I'm here. Until I have the answers I seek, I need to stay alive.

If I have to do this, I'll do it my way. I won't fight, but I will win in the end. I'll let him fuck me, treat me like a breeding cow, until I get my chance to escape—and then I *will* escape, no matter what it costs.

Even if it costs what's left of me.

My eyes flashing, mouth pressed into a stubborn slant, I spin away from him, tugging my arm from his grasp, and bend over the raised platform bed. I present myself ass up in the air and flip up the thin shirt.

Silence meets my action.

Good. I've shocked him. I turn so I can see his expression and lift a brow. "Well, let's get on with it. I won't be fertile forever, Commander." Then, I press my face into the strange blankets and the scent of him fills my nose. Strangely spicy, with a leathery undercurrent.

I want to cry, I know I should, but the tears won't come. My face remains clear and dry until I feel his hand on my hip, and my cheeks heat. Once upon a time, before I'd gone to Hollywood to be an actress,

I'd considered having a family. My own had been so thoroughly messed up, I'd wondered what it would be like. I certainly never thought it would be like this.

His hand fists at my hip, biting into the soft flesh. Is it just my imagination or does it tremble? Surely the big, strong, self-assured commander isn't nervous?

"What are you waiting for?" I demand, my voice muffled from the blanket. "Just get it over with."

Gently, he slides the pants down my thighs and they drop to the floor. My ass is naked to him. Shivers run down my spine at being so vulnerable. His palm cradles my hip and his touch is almost reverent in nature.

"It will be easier if you're prepared," he says, his voice husky. Almost pained sounding. "I don't want to hurt you."

I nearly snort. He's packing some heat in that department, but I didn't think it would matter to him whether or not it would hurt me. He certainly has no problem fucking me for his benefit.

"Just get it over with," I repeat harshly.

The heat of him scorches the back of my legs as he steps closer to me. From that weird sunroom of theirs? The shock of it causes me to shiver and I press my face more fully into the blanket to block out my surroundings. This is just another scene with a faceless actor. I just need to play my part until it's over.

The commander is silent behind me as he pushes the shirt farther up my back. He lifts my hips, then presses a hand to the middle of my shoulder blades, arching my bottom half up to receive him. One of his feet pushes my own out, spreading them enough that he can step between. My breath catches as I feel him moving between my legs, stroking himself.

One hand still between my shoulders, the other gripping his dick, he starts pressing into me. I make a sound in my throat at the size. I'm in no way ready to take him. Nothing about this situation is remotely sexy and even with a normal man, I need to be high as hell to relax enough for any sort of sex. Maybe it will turn him off so much he'll forget about this breeding deal and they'll leave me to my own devices.

He makes a harsh sound and pulls back.

For a second, I'm relieved. Hope spurts quick and hot inside of me. I start to raise up, but the hand at my back stops me.

"What are you doing?" I ask.

Then I feel it.

The head of him brushes against my sex, sending shocks of pleasure and surprise throughout my system. It steals a gasp from my chest and I'm at a loss for words. It feels good, of all things. He reaches a hand around to palm the heavy weight of my breast through the material of the shirt.

"You don't have to do that." My cheeks burn in shame from the breathiness of my tone. How many years have I been subjected to the sexual abuse and harassment that come with my industry? You'd think I would have lost the ability to feel shame at all, but it comes back a million-fold as he works his dick back and forth against my clit.

"Quiet, Aria." Is it just me or does his voice sound harsh? Is it with desire? Irritation?

Desire would work in my favor. Maybe that's why he suggested sex with me instead of simply having them overpower me and return me to cryosleep. Maybe...maybe he really does want me.

It gets harder and harder to think the longer he spends thrusting against me. I reach blindly and find a thin foam sheet that must serve as a pillow and shove my face in it to blot everything out. But it's a fruitless effort because he keeps me in this moment with him. The hand on my back turns soft, reverent. It moves to my hair and rakes through it slowly, and I imagine him staring at it in wonder. My body is nothing like what he's used to and it shows, because he spends the whole time exploring. The rough pads of his fingers scrape along my skin, investigating my shape, all the dips and crevices.

When he's certain I'm ready, those hands travel back down to my hips and I freeze. I want him to want me, because desire makes you do stupid things, but at the same time it's hard for me to let go. *Give him what he wants, Aria. You've done it before.*

His fingers reach my swollen and throbbing clit and then dip farther down and find my entrance. I'm not quite as aroused as he'd like—definitely not enough to take him—so he adds his fingers, the sharpness of his claw scraping along my insides. Tremors ripple through me. I'm so vulnerable. If he truly wanted to, he could gut me simply with his hand.

"Your claws," I whimper, fear making my voice shake.

"I can retract them," he assures me softly.

Thank God for that.

He makes good on his word and the sharpness is suddenly gone, taking some of the terror along with them.

"Too rough, slow down," I tell him, emboldened now that I'm not afraid he'll hurt me.

"This will help," he says as he strokes me from within.

"Not if you're trying to turn me on. You're being

too rough. Go slower, a little softer." I take a deep breath, but it's like trying to inhale soup. I have to do this. "Like this."

I reach down my own hand and cup his strange, bony fingers and show him how to stroke me to life. On the outside. Pulling his fingers out of my body, I guide his hand to the spot that will help me feel good. His claws have indeed disappeared and it's just his firm fingers touching me now.

I can't watch him, can't watch what I'm doing, but he's a quick learner and soon brushes my hand away to take over. And God, now that he knows what I need, he strums me like it's his only goal in life. Like I'm a mist of flora and he wants to consume every bit of me.

There's only so much resisting I can do when I've been surrounded by so much stress. The siren call of pleasure is irresistible. The commander hums in his throat, pleased. His fingers push inside of me briefly, much easier this time, and he quickly pulls them back out.

Now that he's satisfied by my readiness, he aligns with my entrance and pushes his cock inside of me. I raise up on my forearms to turn back and look at him, but he isn't even watching me. His head is thrown back, cheeks flushed—if you can imagine that, considering his complexion. He doesn't sweat, but that same odd flush is spreading over his chest.

The foreplay was pleasurable enough to get me ready to take the bulbous head of his dick, but I know it's the thick length that will be the real challenge. Despite his overall brash attitude, Commander Breccan has incredible patience. He slowly thrusts back and forth, inch by inch, until he's seated inside me.

I don't know what to feel—and for the first time in my life, I don't know how to act. I settle on numb. Numb means whatever happens to me won't affect me. Especially not the fact that I've never been so filled in my life.

He reaches up to palm my breasts again, his claws back out and gently scraping against my flesh. I gasp at how sensitive I've become. At my sound, Breccan slides his palms to my hips and pumps into me harder, his prized control snapping. He thrusts wildly, and even if I were the best actress on the planet, I wouldn't have been able to act like that thick cock spearing into me doesn't affect me. He reaches a place in me I've never felt before, and it tears animal sounds from my chest with each thrust.

He obviously has no problem enjoying it. But I won't. I breathe through it as long as I can, focusing on everything but the way he moves in and out of me. He takes longer than I thought he would to come, but when he does, I breathe a sigh of relief.

Until the heat of his semen spurts inside me, and I lose the ability to move at all.

[5]

BRECCAN

My toxica has entered her bloodstream. I know the moment it happens because my stiff alien relaxes and falls against the bed. A whimper in her throat is the only indication of her distress.

I must work fast to remedy this.

Not even stopping to towel off my cock, I sit on the bed and pull her limp body into my arms. Our species, when breeding, have toxins that are released with our semen that immobilize the female and create a barrier within her to keep the male's seed from spilling out. Those first few moments are critical if implantation is to occur.

"Breathe, little alien," I murmur, running a clawed finger along her hairline, pulling stray strands from her eyes. Her brown eyes are wide and keep darting all around. She's panicking. I should call Avrell to bring something to calm her but I can't risk introducing anything foreign into her body while she's taking my seed.

I will have to calm her the old way. The way of my people. I've heard plenty of stories of females growing terrified their first time. And if I'm being frank with myself, I believe I'd be quite unhappy if the first time I bred with someone, I couldn't move a muscle.

She's nearly completely paralyzed.

And will be for quite some time.

It would behoove her to take a nap.

Her wild eyes that remind me so much of Draven's indicate otherwise. A nap is far from what's on her agenda.

"It's the toxica," I try to explain.

Another hoarse whine rasps from her throat.

"Don't worry," I assure her. "It won't kill you. It's simply rendered you useless so you can accept my seed."

She squeezes her eyes shut and tears leak from the corners. In this moment, my chest feels hollow. As though an unseen force has reached inside me and scooped my insides out.

Leaning forward, I press my forehead to hers. It was something I remembered seeing my father do to my mother when I was young. An unspoken vow. A small display of affection. If my mother was fretting over a meal she was cooking, my father would stride over to her, collect her in his arms, and press his forehead to hers. Immediately, she would calm.

This close, I can smell Aria. She smells unlike anything I can place. A scent that does not exist in our facility. A scent that is unique just to her despite the cleansings Avrell has given to her on multiple occasions.

I inhale her and then breathe out my words. "I will take care of you. This is what our people do. We breed and the males look after their females. "I will protect you as we work together to create our offspring. And once you have one in your womb, I will keep you fed and healthy. You will want for nothing. My little alien, you won't have to lift a finger. I will care for you as dutifully as I do my entire faction here. More so because you are mine."

Lifting slightly, I look into her eyes that have now reopened. They are red, tiny veins crackling away from the irises, from her tears. Her flesh is wet and the overwhelming urge to clean the tears away steals over me.

Calix would lose his mind over what I want to do.

The craving is intense—like that of my need for the UV rays.

It tugs at my nerve endings. Sings songs that beg for me to follow through.

I give in, because my self-control is nearly nonexistent, and I dart out my forked tongue. My tongue runs along the wet trail of her tears, drawing out another fearful sound from her.

She tastes divine.

Unlike anything I've ever tasted.

The urge to lick her again wins over and I find myself tilting her nog this way and that as I clean away her tears. Eventually, I pull away and let out a heavy sigh.

"I like the way you taste," I admit, confusion pulling my brows together. I certainly don't remember my father licking my mother. I'll have to bring this up to Avrell.

She blinks at me but she's no longer crying. Her eyes slowly skim across my features as she studies me. I wonder if she sees me as a strong, worthy mate. One fierce and formidable enough to protect her young. I flatten my ears and let loose a violent, guttural growl to impress her. It should appear fearsome to all.

Another whimpering sound escapes and her eyes are once more darting back and forth. I've upset her again. I try the forehead press again. I lick her even though her tears are dry. I murmur explanations lowly to her. I stroke her hair.

"Y-You." Her word is thick and sludgy in her throat.

I run a claw along her bottom lip and tug it down. "It will come back slowly. The ability to speak and move. That's it," I coo, my claw clinking across her rounded teeth.

She moves her nog slightly to the side, away from me, her eyes looking elsewhere. I don't like that. Clutching her jaw, I bring her to face me again. I shake my nog at her and her nostrils flare. The brown speckles on her cheek are soon joined with red splotches. That, coupled with the furious glint in her eyes, makes me wonder if she's about to attack. I pick up her hand and inspect her useless claws. Her teeth and claws are worthless. Unless she spits out acid, I don't see what her little alien body can do to attack mine.

"If we have a son, I shall name him Sokko after my father," I tell her proudly. "Lania after my mother if it is a girl." I beam at her.

She slowly pulls her weak hand from my grip and reaches it up to my face. I crave her touch and close my eyes. So often, my mother would caress my father's cheeks and—

"Rekk!" I roar when pain rips along my scalp.

Her fingers are tangled in my mane and she keeps yanking on it. I grip her delicate wrist that's nothing but bones wrapped in her pink skin and untangle her grip from my hair.

"No," I bite out, my ears flattening against my nog. "Don't make me restrain you."

She spits at me and I recoil, pushing her away from me as I retreat to one side of the bed. I swipe away her secret venom, hoping I don't lose my sight. It takes a second to realize it's harmless fluid. Like her tears. I dart my tongue out and lap at the sweetness.

"You're a m-monster," she murmurs, her words getting better with each breath.

Her words mean nothing to me as I prowl back toward her, desperate for another taste. That sweet flavor makes my nerve endings come alive. A shriek escapes her when my hard body presses against her soft one. My cock is hard and weeping once more but it'll have to wait. Her body is still performing its protective duties and it's unsafe to enter her again. But that's not what I desire anyhow.

I want inside her mouth.

I want to lick that nectar straight from her tongue.

I need it. I rekking need it.

"P-Please," she whimpers.

I do not know what it is she begs for. All I know is the intense yearning that thrums through me. Her vicious hand that still has strands of my hair twisted around her fingers is a problem and considered a threat. I pin it to the bed as I seek out her mouth. My cock rubs against her pelvis, causing her to make more sounds. The good sounds. The sounds that make me think she's appreciative to have me as a mate.

"I need to taste inside your mouth," I rumble as my forked tongue darts out and teases her pink lips, begging her for access.

In a petulant way that reminds me of Hadrian when he was younger, she presses her mouth into a firm line. Fire ignites within me and I wonder why she is choosing to be difficult.

I will coax her to open her mouth for me.

Just like I coaxed her cunt to grow wet for me.

And just like then, when I rub my cock between her lower lips, she lets out garbled sounds that drive me to the brink of madness. Slowly, in a teasing way, I slide my cock against her pleasure spot. Rubbing and rubbing and rubbing. It's like a hot button to turn her to mush. I love this button. Perhaps one solar, I'll see if my tongue works on this button. Until that solar, I will use my cock.

"You like when I rub you here," I tell her, a cocky smirk on my face. I like it too. Everywhere I touch her brings me pleasure.

She glowers at me and I chuckle. For such a miniature alien, she's so fierce. Pride surges through me. I'm lucky to have gotten such a strong one for a mate. She's worthy of a tough commander.

"When your cunt is ready again, I'm going to slip inside you and deliver more of my seed," I murmur. "I'll keep you beneath me just like this until it takes."

"You can't do that," she chokes out.

Impressed at my ability to make her speak, I choose the moment not to reply but to taste her sweetness. She lets out a sound of surprise when I push my tongue into her mouth. It's longer than hers, so I'm able to really delve inside. The burst of flavor on my tongue makes me groan. My double fangs threaten to slice her small tongue, but I'm mindful because she is precious and I don't want to hurt her. Between the way I'm rubbing against her and getting high on her taste, I'm going to spill my seed if I'm not careful.

I'm losing my grip on my sanity, losing myself to her, when a violent explosion runs up my tongue.

She bit me!

Blood drips from my mouth and onto her face. I stare at her in horror. How dare she! How are her dulled teeth worth anything?

She bares her teeth at me, smeared with my blood, the wildness in her eyes shocking me. Her body is still weak from the toxica but there is strength in her expression. In her actions.

I reach up and touch one of her teeth. Not nearly as sharp as my double fangs, but pointy enough to pierce soft flesh, apparently.

All anger leeches from me as I admire her. Her tea-colored hair fans out over my bed coverings and I decide she's beautiful. Like the sun I desperately crave. She is the sun as well. Perhaps I even prefer looking at her over the burning mass.

I pin both her wrists and stare down at her, my cock sliding once more against her pleasure spot. She desperately holds on to her anger but soon her lashes are fluttering. Sweet whimpers of need escape. And if I were able to finger her cunt without risking the potential implantation, I'd know she was slick with her arousal.

"You're a worthy mate," I croon, a smile tugging at my lips. "Strong. A commander's equal."

I capture her wrists with one hand and use my claw to pierce her shirt at the top and then drag it down, slicing through the material. Jareth will have a fit knowing I've destroyed precious garments but I can't even bring myself to care. Not when I'm opening my mate up to me like a gift. I pull away the material to reveal her breasts. A handful and perky. They will fill with milk and feed our mortling well. The pride surging through me is overwhelming.

Oh the luck!

"So beautiful," I murmur. "So strong." I grin at her. "Mine."

I rut against her again, careful to not accidentally penetrate. Now that the toxica is wearing off, she begins squirming. Not attempting to escape me but rocking with me in effort to seek out more pleasure. I rotate my hips, rubbing circles on her sweet spot as I flick her hardened nipple with my claw. It rises higher at my touch. One solar it will leak with nourishment. My cock twitches as I wonder if that too will taste so wonderful.

"Breccan," she whispers, no longer angry. My name on her lips is a reward. A reward for this horrible life I've been sentenced to. In one word, she erases it all. The death. Our uninhabitable world. The loneliness.

My little alien is a fixer.

A cure for the madness.

She is my gift.

Her body trembles as I bring her closer to pleasure. Those plump lips of hers part. I'm hungry for another taste but I will wait until her mood improves. Perhaps after I've made her come undone.

"Ah!" Her back arches off the bed and her breasts jiggle as she cries out. I'm fascinated by her reactions. I want to learn everything there is to know about her.

I will because she is mine.

When she spirals back down, I slide beside her, releasing her hands. She watches me with furrowed brows as I rake my claws through her hair. I will take care of her. Soon, she will realize this. Soon, it will become known to her and she will trust me.

I am her mate now.

My entire happiness revolves around her.

And the moment I'm forced to go back to work, I'm going to send Theron and Sayer to procure us more of these fine aliens.

Every single mort of mine will have one.

I'll see to that if it's the last thing I do.

[6]
ARIA

THE FUCKER PARALYZED ME. Paralyzed!

I can't believe it, even though my limbs are still heavy and slow to respond to the simplest of commands. Breccan—I can't think of him as the commander, now that he's been inside me—has to carry me back out of his room and to the medical area for observation. It took me awhile just for me to be able to function enough to move again.

"It won't always take so long for you to recover, little one. Your body should acclimate to the toxica. I'll confirm this with Avrell."

"Fuck you," I spit.

I'm still pissed. Not because of the paralyzing, though trust me, that's high up there on my list of complaints.

I'm pissed about how much I enjoyed it.

Being unable to move heightened the pleasure to a point where I nearly lost consciousness. I couldn't escape from it, there was nowhere to go. All I could do was take it.

And now all I want to do is take it again and again.

He's more addictive than the strongest drug.

And more dangerous.

"I don't know what this means." His strong arms flex underneath me as he opens the door to Avrell's office.

Sensing an opportunity to get some much-needed space, I throw myself from his arms. "It means...whatever. Just leave me alone." I storm into the examination room and jump up on the table. I can only assume they want to make sure their implantation was a success, and I'd rather get the humiliation over with as soon as possible so I can go back to our room and fall asleep. At least then, I won't have to face how completely screwed up everything is.

Avrell looks up from the computer screen where he's working. On the screen in front of him, I observe pictures of other women in cryosleep. There are four of them.

Then it occurs to me.

I can't leave these women behind. I can't let them

face this fate if I can do something to save them. In addition to saving myself, I'll have to figure out a way to save them, too.

Avrell closes out of the screen before I can determine anything else.

That's fine. I've got nothing but time to figure out where they're keeping the girls and a plan to get us all out of here before we become a breeding harem for these monsters.

I still can't quite decipher their expressions as easily as I could if they were human, but if I had to hazard a guess, I'd say Avrell is surprised we're back so soon.

"You've copulated already?" He takes a scanning wand from his pocket and crosses the room to me. I lean back on the examination table as he waves it over me. Exhaustion crashes over me in waves and the lethargy from the paralysis doesn't help.

I crack an eye open to see Breccan practically preening. "Aria had a severe reaction to the toxica. Will you scan to see if there are any complications?"

Avrell sighs in resignation as he turns away from Breccan. "I told you the likelihood this would work is slim. If you damaged her when we could have used her for incubation instead—"

Breccan's responding growl fills the room and I

mimic Avrell's sigh. I think sometimes he likes to hear his own superiority.

"Just scan her!" His strange tapered ears flatten against his skull and his eyeteeth extend past his lips like some kind of emo vampire. A *hot* one, though I'd never admit it.

Avrell waves the scanner over my body as it beeps and transmits information to the screen. I can't read their odd language, but I do recognize a readout of my body and the corresponding components. Not that I know what any of it means. I glance at Breccan as he steps closer to my side, a deep rumble still emanating from his chest.

"Relax. Why are you being so protective, Commander? I'm just scanning her, as ordered." He sends Breccan a knowing look, who glances away, finally going quiet.

"Since this is my body we're talking about, will you tell me what's going on and why you're checking me? I thought you said the toxica was safe." It certainly didn't feel safe being paralyzed. More like frightening. I thought cryosleep was terrifying, but being so vulnerable in this strange place full of intimidating males isn't exactly my idea of a reprieve. Especially not with Breccan, who has made me so conflicted in such a short period of time.

Avrell finishes scanning and swipes through the screen at the bedside. "The toxica is safe. Paralysis during first-time copulation is usually the worst it'll ever be. It'll lessen as your body grows accustomed to the toxica. The recovery time will shorten and your faculties will return much more quickly while your body's ability to retain our seed will increase with each exposure." He smiles at me. "I'm checking to see if—"

There's a quick knock at the door and then another alien appears, though this one looks much younger than Breccan and Avrell. His face is unlined and his hair looks as untamed as his smile. It reminds me of those sharply angled Goth haircuts teenagers used to sport when I was younger. It works on his face, which is cut with dramatic cheekbones and a slashing brow. His pointed ears twitch when his eyes land on me and his eyes crinkle as he breaks into a wide, youthful smile.

"Hadrian. You should be in the command center attending to your duties," Breccan says sharply. He moves closer to me as Hadrian advances, nonplussed by Breccan's admonishment.

"Draven took over for a while so I could do a perimeter check. During my rounds, I saw the light on here and decided to check to make sure no help was needed." He speaks at double speed and fidgets in place as though he has the energy of a toddler. "Is she breeding yet, Av? Can you tell?"

Despite everything, his exuberance makes me want to smile because it's so uncalculated. He reminds me of me when I was younger. Innocent. Untainted by the miseries and pressures of life.

"Hadrian!" Avrell says sharply, but I lift a heavy arm to touch Avrell's hand.

"It's all right," I say, but Breccan is practically vibrating next to me. Avrell wisely moves out of my reach. My hand drops back to the bed. Breccan bristles but settles down. "Well," I say to Avrell. "You may as well answer him. That's why we're all here, isn't it?"

Breccan, if at all possible, crowds closer. He tries to take my hand but I evade him. The last thing I want is to be close to him right now.

Avrell swipes at the screen, makes notes and checks readings. I have no idea how they're able to tell if I'm pregnant after just one time, let alone so quickly, but they must be able to. He turns to Breccan. "I'm sorry, Commander. Not this time."

I expect Breccan to react badly, but he seems... pleased by this news. It's evident he enjoyed sleeping with me. Probably more than I realize.

Which could work for my plan of escape. I'll woo him with my tricks in bed, let him think I'm being compliant, and then disappear from right beneath his should-be-ugly-but-isn't nose.

"Can I speak to you in private?" Avrell asks Breccan, who nods and follows him out of the examination room.

"Rekk, you're beautiful," Hadrian blurts. "For an alien, I mean."

He's disarmingly charming and his blunt comments make me like him more than I should. "You don't look too bad yourself—for an alien," I respond, and then smile to let him know I didn't take any offense. "So you work in the command center? Is that far from here?" Despite how much I like him, it occurs to me Hadrian's youthful ignorance can also be an advantage. The layout is confusing to me and learning what I can about the place will be helpful.

"It's on the south side of the facility."

"What do you do there?"

Hadrian sits on the bed next to me, but his foot taps against the ground. "I'm in training to become the next commander. I'll take Breccan's place when he ages out." He turns to me, his face growing serious. "If he makes it that far. It's been a long time since a mort aged out. Most of our people die from worse things than old age."

That I can imagine, and I haven't even seen the

world outside their facility. If they're resorting to breeding with humans, it is no surprise the place is dangerous. "What happened to your people? To your parents? How many of you are left?"

"Rekk, a ton of things. Disease. Droughts. Geostorms. Sabrevipes. Mortuus is a dangerous planet and only the strongest morts have survived. There are ten of us in all. Only males, which is why it's so fortunate that you're here."

I notice he didn't answer my question about his parents, and I don't press.

Hadrian leaps to his feet when Avrell and Breccan return. "I better get back to my rounds." Then he's through the sliding door and off before any of us can respond.

I hope I wasn't terribly insensitive with my questioning, and despite my loathing for this place and Breccan, I'll make it a point to apologize to him if I was.

"Well, Doc, what do we do now?"

"We try again," Breccan growls.

My heart sinks. I knew that would be the case, but I was hoping for a different outcome.

Breccan makes a move to grab me and leave, but Avrell stops him. "I'll have a word with Aria before you go. Alone." Before Breccan can growl, Avrell assures him it'll only be a minute.

As soon as Breccan has stepped into the hallway, Avrell says, "I noticed you did something to Breccan's tongue. We were curious if this was an alien custom."

Mind blank, I can only blink at him. "Something to his...oh, you mean when I bit him?" Laughter bubbles up and spills over. "God, no. I was just pissed—angry— when he paralyzed me. It's not a custom."

Avrell's shoulders relax, but his expression is still serious. "Good. But I'd prefer if you didn't repeat that again. Open wounds spread disease and disease here can be fatal. Even the slightest wound could be catastrophic."

"Is he going to be okay?" I don't ask out of concern... not for him, anyway. I ask because even though he's a monster, he's the only monster here I know. Leaving me to another—potentially one who's even more dangerous —isn't an outcome I'd considered until now. So much for my plan to hurt him if it ever came down to it.

"He'll be fine. I attended to the wound with microbots—tiny robots programmed to repair wounds."

I have more questions about the microbots, but Breccan appears, impatient, in the doorway. Time to leave.

"Thank you, Avrell," because I don't know what else to say.

"Good solar to you, Aria," he responds, but he's already back to squinting at the screens.

I sigh and follow Breccan back through the hallways to our room. This time, I dress and climb into bed without questioning. I'm so tired I couldn't care where I lie or with who. Tomorrow, I'll deal with what happened to me. Tomorrow, I'll deal with the adoring way Breccan looks at me. For now, I just want to get through tonight.

He settles behind me, wrapping me in his limbs until I'm surrounded by a cage of them. His warmth envelops me, attempts to comfort me, but I don't let it. It doesn't take long for the big guy to fall asleep.

As soon as he does, his heavy arm and thickly muscled thigh slung atop my sore and well-used body, I throw myself from the bed. There is no way I'll be able to sleep with him. I don't want to be anywhere near him.

I steal a large shirt from the clothing cabinets and wrap it around me like a blanket. With my arm for a pillow as I curl up on the cold floor, I drop into a deep and dreamless sleep.

It's not the sirens that wake me, but the weight of a

full-grown alien on top of me, his ears flat against his head and a growl reverberating in his chest. "Sabre-vipes," he warns. "Attacking the facility. Stay here. Don't leave this room."

[7]
BRECCAN

THE SIRENS ARE BLASTING as I rush to shrug on my protective gear over my minnasuit. I've called Draven, Jareth, and Theron to my aid as they are my most skilled fighters. When Hadrian pops up and starts putting on his suit, I roar, "Stay!"

"No," he argues, donning his gear quicker than the rest of us. "I've been training to do this. I can help kill them. I'm quicker than any of you old morts!" He grins before pulling a mask over his nog.

I don't have time to argue so I grunt instead. He better not get himself rekking killed because I'm not sure I'm mentally equipped to deal with a loss like that. But as much as I want to keep him caged away and protected like when he was young, he'll never learn if I don't let him loose from time to time. I snatch my sharpest and longest magknife, one that's slaughtered many a sabrevipe. Draven picks up a spear that Ozias made. It's pointed like a normal arrow but once it pierces its target, five blades shoot out so as you pull it back out, it shreds everything upon exit. It's lethal, and Draven has proven to be the most skilled at it.

Theron grabs his zonnoblaster, something that's proven useful when we need to get away in a pinch. It blasts a spray of titanium slugs that melt and expand upon penetrating flesh. Incredibly painful. Ozias almost lost his foot when he accidentally shot himself once.

Jareth, like me, prefers blades. His are smaller and he likes one in each hand. The mort is quite skilled at throwing them. I've seen him throw them as far as the eye can see and still hit the target right where he'd intended.

That brings us to Hadrian.

I don't know what the mortarekking gods he'll use. He rummages around in the weapon closet though and produces several items. As soon as everyone is dressed in protective gear and ready to fight, I type in the sixteen-digit code and we rush out into the elements.

"Attacking the north side," Sayer radios in. "I see you on the radar emerging from the west entrance. Be careful. The winds are high and there are at least six sabrevipes clawing at that door."

"Copy that," I say back as I motion for my men to follow.

We creep along the rocky side of our facility, our weapons drawn. The winds are so furious that my mask keeps moving. Alarm sends my heart skipping twice as fast. I don't have a second to think about the fact that alien Aria is not pregnant. I'd been eager to mate with her again this solar but then everything went to rogshite.

I point at Draven and then motion ahead. He's quiet and stealthy. Hadrian, the loud mortarekker, can stay to the rear. The last thing I need is for him to draw their attention before we're ready.

Draven prowls forward, soundlessly, with his spear poised and ready. I gesture for Jareth and Theron to proceed ahead of me. They take their cue and move forward as well. Hadrian is being surprisingly quiet and vigilant, which has pride thumping through me.

That's my boy.

"Two have turned and are heading west," Sayer warns. "Keep your rekking eyes peeled."

Before I can warn Draven, a sabrevipe peeks his nog around the corner. The nog of the sabrevipe is about the size of five mort nogs put together. Three pale blue eyes, the middle one milky and clouded over. Nostrils that are flat against its head and as big around as my fist. Long whiskers that move of their own accord, tasting the air for the scent of its prey. But the most fearsome thing about sabrevipes are their teeth.

As if on cue, the feral animal opens its mouth and roars. Menacing and ferocious. I can feel the vibrations all the way down to my toes.

We all remain frozen, as it's best to wait for them to attack. Sometimes they will show their vulnerabilities to us that way. This one, much larger than the one who cowers behind it, stands on its hind legs. It's as tall as Draven, if he stood on my shoulders. Sharp, silvery claws catch the sunlight off to the west, opposite of the incoming geostorm, and nearly blind me. Their claws are every bit as lethal as our blades.

"Now!" I yell.

Draven rushes forward without hesitation, his arm rearing back. He gets close, but not too close, and releases the spear. It spirals straight ahead, stabbing right through the hairless animal's belly, just below its heart.

The sabrevipe screams and when it lands on all fours, the spear pushes deeper and pokes through near its spine. But until Draven grabs hold and yanks it back, the spear's intended purpose is useless.

The cowering sabrevipe that I can now tell is a baby takes off running back to the north side.

"Get it!" I yell to Theron and Jareth.

But before they can go, Hadrian takes off in a sprint.

Mortarekker!

Theron and Jareth run after him while I help Draven take down the big one that's swiping its massive clawed paw at him. He pulls his magknife from his leg strap and holds it out in front of him.

"Any others?" I bellow to Sayer through the radio.

"Negative," he replies. They took off because the geostorm is intensifying. Ran off to the caves by Lake Acido."

"Good," I growl as I stalk around the side of the sabrevipe, making a wide arc. Draven is distracting it and angering it by kicking rocks its way. It's bleeding out and furious but keeping its distance.

The animal's tail lashes back and forth and I'm careful to not step on it as I near. Not wasting any time, I charge and launch myself on its back, mindful of where the spear protrudes. My magknife plunges deep into its side between its ribs. A scream of pain from the animal makes the mountain rumble in response.

But it takes a moment to realize that it's not the rumbling of the mountain...but thunder instead.

Rekk!

Water droplets pelt the glass of my mask, making it more difficult to see. The storm picks up and the animal tries to fight back. But I am quicker. I've already pulled the magknife out and stabbed it again. It stands on its hind legs again as if to shake me off.

It will be its fatal mistake.

Draven roars and rushes forward. He grabs his spear and yanks.

Crunching and tearing can be heard as the weapon works as intended. It shreds and yanks vital organs as he pulls it back out. The animal goes limp beneath me and collapses to the rocky earth below.

A high-pitched screaming can be heard, and I know it's the smaller sabrevipe nearby. Draven nods at me that he's got this one, and I climb off the animal to sprint to check on my men. When I round the corner, I see its tail lashing from behind a rock but neither Theron or Jareth are moving forward.

"What are you waiting for?" I demand.

"He's got Hadrian trapped. I think it's frightened and doesn't know where to go," Jareth explains.

My chest feels as though it's crushing in on itself. Not Hadrian. He's like my own mortling, that one. I'd die protecting that boy. He may be every bit as tall as me now and quite the fighter, but he'll always be the mortling who required me to change his soiled undersuits.

Rekk!

What was I thinking? He's not ready. Too impulsive and out of control. He'll never be a leader like he wants while he behaves like this.

He's not dying.

Not on my watch.

I launch forward and climb up the rocky side to see if I can get a look down in the area where the sabre-vipe has him trapped. Once I climb to the top, I see that it has him pinned. It keeps tearing at his zu-gear, shredding through the tough material as though it's nothing. My breath is sucked from my chest. It will puncture his minnasuit underneath and there's no telling what sort of impurities will get in his system. The last thing I need is my youngest mort catching The Rades. He'd never survive it. Draven hardly did and he's twice his size.

"Hadrian," I bellow.

"I'm okay," he yells back. "Rekk, this sabe is heavy!"

The sabrevipe lifts its nog and all three of its eyes blink at me. Fear flickers in the young one's gaze but I don't let it sway my decision. It's either this animal or Hadrian. I'll always choose my men over that of the rotten landscape and what dwells on it.

I jump down into the crevasse, landing on the animal's back. It screeches but I don't give it time to react. I dig my magknife into its throat and rip from ear to ear. A hiss and a splash indicate I've hit all its fatal arteries and it crashes against Hadrian.

Hadrian groans and twitches beneath it. The rekker is too heavy to pull off on my own but thankfully Theron squeezes in beside me. Together, we drag the beast off my boy and out of the crevice.

Jareth rushes inside and helps Hadrian to his feet. Immediately, he pulls out the sealatape and begins patching the holes in his suit. In this world, there is no time for waiting. No margin for error. He needs to seal any holes before harmful bacteria or pathogens get in. I hope it isn't too late.

As we drag the animal out into the open, more wind and rain from the worsening geostorm pelt us. The winds are strong and it's nearly rekking impossible to drag the heavy sabrevipe and push against the storm. Slowly, we make our way forward and eventually meet up with Draven. Hadrian and Jareth move to help him since that animal is larger. All five of us carry our haul to the west entrance. By the time we get there,

Sayer is waiting with the door open, his protective gear in place. He assists us and we drag the carcasses into the decontamination bay once inside. We use the bigger bay for our kills, and there is a smaller one where we morts go.

Once we're all sealed inside the smaller room, Sayer punches some buttons on the wall. Purified, pressurized water bursts from six directions. All four walls, floor, and ceiling. It cleanses us of the elements and filth. Then, the second phase begins. Air, as hard and furious as a geostorm, blasts from the ceiling. We all hold on to the harnesses along the wall to keep from toppling over. Another round of water rinses us again.

The third phase is a chemical agent Calix designed. It coats us like rain from the ceiling, slick and sludgy. According to him, it attacks any lingering pathogens. Once we sit for a few seconds to let that do its job, more water. Then, air. A loud beep indicates we're thoroughly cleansed.

We don't always go through the latter heavy phase of decontamination, like in the case of unloading Theron and Sayer's hauls, but after hunting missions or any of Galen's trips where we're exposed for long periods, we do. Especially if blood is involved.

Calix, all dressed in protective gear, waits on the

other side of the door when it reopens. "Hadrian, come with me."

Jareth must have radioed in to let him know his suit was torn and he was exposed. Since Calix is our contagious diseases specialist, he'll make sure Hadrian isn't at risk for anything lethal.

"You almost got yourself killed out there," I grumble to Hadrian.

He beams at me from behind his mask. "Still alive, old mort. Still alive." He makes horn symbols with his gloved hands and a smile tugs at my lips. When he was smaller and couldn't speak just yet, he wanted me to show him books of rogcows—animals that are rare but taste rekking delicious when charred right. That was his way of communicating that he wanted to see pictures of his favorite animal. Now, he likes to flash me his rogcow symbols, as if trying to remind me he's as spectacular as one of those much-coveted animals.

"Go on, you piece of rogshite." I shake my nog and pat his shoulder as he walks by. "I want a full report immediately."

"On it, Commander," Calix assures me. He knows how much Hadrian means to me. "The kills have been cleared as well."

I give him a pleased nod that the sabrevipes are safe to eat.

"Draven, you got this?" I ask as we file out of the small decontamination bay.

He gives me a nod. While the rest of us start removing our gear, he remains in his to go skin and cut up the sabrevipes. Galen, who is an excellent cook, will be pleased we were able to kill two and that they are edible. Often, we manage to kill one, only to discover it's diseased. Such a waste. But this solar, we will sleep with our bellies filled.

Speaking of filled bellies...

Exhaustion seeps through my bones. I want to curl up with my mate and hold her. Her scent is like a powerful agent that helps me sleep. The many benefits of having this little alien are not lost on me. She should be pleased at my kills this solar and will most likely be eager for my seed. *Should* being the key word here. My little alien surprises me often and doesn't seem to be impressed like she should be at my efforts. Perhaps I shall try harder.

I let out a yawn as I drag toward my quarters.

Later.

I will regale her of the tale of our brave hunt, push my cock into her, and gift her my seed later.

First, a nap.

As I walk past the command center, I twitch to go

inside. But I'm pulled in the direction of Aria, equally so. For a moment, indecision renders me still.

We will partake of the UV time together, then.

A wide grin tugs at my lips.

I can have both at once.

My cock twitches in my minnasuit.

What a reward for a taxing solar.

I'm coming, little alien, and rekk, do I have a treat for you.

[8]
ARIA

THE ROOM around me is in ruins.

Clothes, blankets, and his weird slithery suits that make his body look killer litter the floor in a wild tangle. The tubes of cream and gel I found in his bathroom pool in the sink. I didn't recognize any of the concoctions, but I uncapped them and spilled them out anyway, hoping to find something useful.

I should feel guilty about wrecking all of Breccan's belongings, but all I have to do to motivate me to not give a damn is remember how it felt to be powerless beneath him or recall the faces of the other women on Avrell's screen.

After an hour—who knows, I have no watch—of ripping through all his storage cabinets, investigating the walls' points of weakness and scouring the side rooms accessible through sliding panels, I've found nothing of use. The facility itself is impenetrable. They *want* to be locked up tight within these walls based on what Hadrian told me about their harsh planet.

Agreeing to be their breeder was a mistake of epic proportions. I've made some shitty decisions in my life, but sleeping with an alien has to be in my top five.

Escaping while they were gone fighting whatever monstrous beings inhabit this planet would have been the perfect plan. If I only could have figured out a way to get out of the room. I'm not sure I would have been in a huge hurry to go outside, though. A shudder ripples through me as I consider the terrifying planet Hadrian described. I definitely need to come up with a better plan because sneaking out of the building and entering an unsafe world doesn't seem like the best idea.

Now, I lie atop the mountain of clothes, defeated. I can't get out of the room without an armband or the code they type into the panel. Exhausted and over-whelmed, I doze, wrapped in Breccan's scent with the memory of his long-clawed hands still inked into my skin like a tattoo. I have a feeling it'll be just as perma-nent. Memories of the way he kissed me—so dominant and consuming—assaults my mind. I'd liked it. For a split second, I loved the way his slick, unusual forked tongue slid against mine and I almost got lost in him. He'd tasted unlike anything I'd ever known but it wasn't bad. Minty is the closest taste I can equate it to. I craved to close my eyes and imagine I was back home making out with a big, beautiful man. But the moment his razor-sharp teeth scraped across mine, a threatening reminder of who he was, I found my resolve and bit him. I'd made him bleed and I think he deserved it.

When I wake again, it's to Breccan on top of me. My first thought is, *Damn, he sure takes this breeding thing seriously.*

My second is that I don't want to be paralyzed again.

He's somehow stripped me without waking me. I'm naked atop his bed, my arms bound by one of his clawed hands above my head. My legs are pinned nearly to my chest and slung over his shoulders, his thick cock rubbing against my clit. Fear has me frozen from the inside out much like the effects of the toxica— the only thing it doesn't block out is how fucking good it feels.

Don't think about it, Aria.

Be strong.

Stop rocking your hips in tandem with him.

But I can't help but think about the way his cock

slides against my sensitive clit. My sole focus is on the expert way he makes my body thrum to life. His rubbing feels too good.

I want him inside me. I want him to stop teasing me and push into me. The thought that I'm craving this monster like a hit of flora is enough to have me questioning my sanity.

Be strong.

An embarrassing, needy moan rumbles from me. This pleases him because he smiles at me. So much for being strong.

"There you are, my little Aria. Come back to me. Does that feel good?"

So good.

"No," I lie, my voice breathy.

A chuckle rumbles from him as he works his hips in a circular way. My body shudders in response as zings of pleasure pulsate from my core to every nerve ending in my body. It's maddening being with him. I work so hard to mentally convince myself what a bad idea this is but I've never felt so alive. He feels good. Too good. It's hard to hate him when he's making me lose my mind as he draws out an orgasm.

Stars glitter around me as I climax. I'm still trembling, overcome with bliss, when he pushes slowly into me. Stretching and filling me to the brink. It heightens the orgasm that's still thrumming through me and I moan in relief at having him fully inside me.

Thrust. Thrust. Thrust.

My core tightens with the need to come again.

Thrust. Thrust. Thrust.

Oh, God.

"Don't worry, I'll take care of you," he murmurs, his voice fierce. "You feel so rekking good. I meant to wait until after I rested, but you clearly missed me too much while I was gone. Your display of your displeasure was thoroughly received. I plan to breed with you tonight for hours to make it up to you."

Thrust. Thrust. Thrust.

He groans when his orgasm rushes from him and into my body. His cock throbs out every venomous drop. No longer needing to hold my arms, thanks to the paralytic effect of his semen, he takes advantage and his claws begin to trace every available inch of my skin. The heavy-lidded look he's giving me infuriates me and I could slap him for making me enjoy this, but I'll have to make do with giving him a death glare.

The slow stroking goes on until he's nearly soft—if you could call it that—and can barely stay inside any longer. He doesn't seem in any hurry to get off me, though, and all I can do is wait it out. Avrell said it would be less and less each time, but now I'm starting to wonder if that was just a line of bullshit they fed me to keep me from freaking out even more.

Wisely, I don't think about what Breccan means by breeding for hours.

When he's done, he runs a hand over his cock to gather the semen dripping from the tip. With his eyes on mine, he carefully rubs at my folds, then presses his slick fingers inside me.

I throw my head back against the bed, the toxica relenting enough for me to moan aloud. Even though I know the why's, even though I know it shouldn't, it still sends shockwaves throughout me.

Breccan's eyes take on a satisfied glint. "Take every last drop, mortania. As soon as you're feeling better, I've got something to show you. I have a feeling you'll enjoy it."

While I lie frozen on the bed, Breccan dresses and then moves around the room cleaning up the mess I'd made without a negative word. Once he's done, he wets a small towel and approaches me. He's gentle and caring as he cleanses me between my thighs, his black eyes intense and on mine. I try to ignore the stirrings in my chest. The happy way in which he takes care of me is confusing. My gut instinct is to hate him but he makes it too hard, especially when he is being so sweet. His hands are reverent as he strokes my flat stomach and the crack in my chest seems to grow wider. Pride and hope glimmer in his stare. There's nothing intimidating or infuriating about him now. Not in this moment. Right now, he's beautiful and regarding me as though I'm his whole world. I've never been anyone's entire world. With a sigh of regret, he finally leaves me to find me something to wear. Even as he dresses me, he does it with careful consideration as though he doesn't want to hurt me.

Damn him for making a mess of my mind.

I forget to be angry when he picks me up for another trek through the facility. "Where are we going?" I ask when my voice returns.

This may be my chance to figure out an escape plan. Or at the very least distract Breccan long enough to get his armband. I feel a twinge of guilt at the thought of betraying him but I can't afford to be weak. These...men have no qualms about using me. I shouldn't have any about using them in return.

He gives me a grin I can only describe as roguish and I have to wonder if getting laid hasn't improved the sour commander's disposition. "The command center."

My biting retort dies in my throat. The command center. "Can you put me down? I can walk."

His gait doesn't slow. "I don't mind carrying you. You're very light for a female of your size."

"A female of my size?"

"You've the hips and breasts for a breeding woman. I'd expected you to weigh much more."

I throw my weight to the side and by a miracle, manage to land on my feet. "What the hell? Are you calling me fat?"

The pronounced brows on his forehead shift in what I think is a quizzical look. "Are you displeased? These will be useful for when you're carrying our young. I don't understand your anger."

Remember the command center. "Forget it," I say from between gritted teeth. "Are we almost there?" I think I've gotten the directions from his quarters to the main run of the facility. We're nearing Avrell's office and the medical bay I remember from before.

"It's just a bit farther south," Breccan answers, but he glances at me as though he can't quite figure me out.

That'll make two of us, buddy.

The command center is empty when we find it and I wonder if Hadrian's shift has ended now that Breccan's here. He slides his armband under the sensor and the doors beep as they slide open. "Welcome, Commander Breccan," says a slightly digitized female voice.

"Good solar to you, Uvie," he greets the voice.

We step inside and Breccan crosses to a wall of computer screens atop a bank of countertops covered in different buttons. As he studies the screens intently, I wander around the room, trying to get my bearings. Immediately across from the doors is the giant window that's now covered with a massive metal door. I've been here before. I remember now. A heat creeps up my throat as I recall the way Breccan had stood in front of the open window that day with the sun shining in on him and he looked high as a kite. Avrell had handed him a cloth to clean himself when we walked in. Talk about awkward. Despite us catching him right after he'd been pleasuring himself, he wasn't ashamed.

Forcing myself to think about other things besides Breccan and his cock, I survey the equipment in the room. Everything, like the rest of the facility is old, but as clean as I've come to expect from these strange males. They've mentioned disease and infection, but I'm coming to realize they take cleanliness to the extreme.

"We can only stay here for a few minutes—your skin is still sensitive yet."

"My skin?" I turn to face Breccan, who has come to stand behind me.

"Here," he says, and starts pulling on the metal door that covers the window. "Let me show you." A horrible scraping bellows from the wall as it opens. I flinch at the loud sound. "Don't fret," he says lowly as he comes to wrap his arms around me from behind. "I will keep you safe."

The window reveals a swirl of light and an intense wave of heat. I didn't realize how cold they kept the facility until the rush of warmth greets my skin and I moan in delight. Behind me, Breccan stiffens and hisses out a breath, but I don't pay much attention because the heat is glorious, almost like a good day at the beach back home. I close my eyes because it's too bright to look out the window anyway and pretend I'm lying on the sand with the sound of waves in my ear and a nice drink by my side.

Minutes pass, I don't know how long. So long my knees ache from standing and my skin itches as though I've gotten a sunburn. It's worth it though, because for the first time, I don't feel so afraid—or so alone.

I turn to Breccan, to thank him or to what, I don't know—but it doesn't matter. His skin has gone a horrible shade of red and the blacks of his eyes have been bleached white. He makes a terrible sound before falling to his knees as his eyes roll back into his head and he crumples to the ground.

For a moment, I panic. Half of me eyes the door. This would be the perfect moment to escape. I cringe as I consider the harsh conditions and creepy animals Hadrian spoke of. Okay, so maybe escape is a bad idea. I push that thought away immediately. Worry over Breccan takes over every thought in my mind.

The moment of indecision over what to do costs me and I do the second-best thing while I have the time.

I close the giant covers for the windows. It takes more effort than I expect and I grunt as I drag it closed, the scraping sound an assault to my eardrums. Breccan's body shakes at my feet, then relaxes as the last rays of sunlight are covered. I take the armband from Breccan's lifeless body without a second thought, then use it to open the door and scream for help into the hallway. Avrell's offices are near. He has to hear me. Then, I store the armband in one of my pockets and go back to Breccan's side to assess the damage.

His skin looks hot to the touch and has already broken out with sores in some places. I'm afraid to touch him, afraid to move him. I wonder as I bring his head into my lap if this is why they wear the suits. I hadn't even realized he'd stripped his down behind me. His whole upper body looks bright red and painful. Is this why their skin is so white? They're not subjected to the sun's rays at all, so they obviously wouldn't get a tan. As I wait for help, it makes me wonder where they came from and what exactly they are.

Breccan begins to come around as I hear footsteps racing down the hall. Relieved, tears sting my eyes as he opens his. "Why didn't you say it was going to hurt you?" I demand. Tears drip down my cheeks and land in his hair.

He raises a welted arm and catches one of the salty offerings to bring to his lips. "It seemed to bring my mate such joy. I didn't want to interrupt."

I feel the first stirrings of...I don't know what. I don't want to know. It reminds me of the way my chest felt inside when we had sex earlier and then how he took care of me after. I hurry to wipe the tears away as Avrell comes to our side. He lifts Breccan with surprising ease and we hurry back to the exam room, where we have been far too many times already.

As he and Breccan discuss what happened, I follow behind, my mind a confused maze.

"We've talked about this," Avrell mutters under his breath to Breccan. "It's getting out of control."

"It's not out of control," Breccan grunts. "I'm fine."

"It's not out of control. I'm fine."

I remember saying those same words to my sister. We'd spoken on the phone and I'd admitted using flora. Instead of moving on, she was concerned about my being addicted to it.

"I'm not addicted."

I'd laughed at her. But it hurt hearing those words. I was completely addicted despite my denial. The only way I could cope with the stress of my job and things that had happened to me was with constant hits of flora. It was more like a nightmare than reality. There, I was an idol, but a mistreated one. I lived for the mind-numbing high. It was my escape.

What is Breccan escaping from?

He practically overdosed on the sun's rays, that much I can gather. So what is it that makes him need to escape?

Responsibility. Hopelessness. Pain.

Again, my chest aches. I can relate. Having the weight of the world on your shoulders is an incredible burden. Back home, I was groomed to look and act, literally, a certain way. I never got to just be.

Like here?

I haven't needed the flora since I've been here. This whole new world has been too big and too scary, but not one I needed to flee mentally from. At first, maybe, I thought it was, but as I spend more time here with these people, I'm realizing that never-ending desire to numb myself doesn't exist.

My mind flits to earlier with Breccan in his bed. I'd been paralyzed but I wasn't numb. I felt the way he pleasured and worshipped me. It wasn't awful. Far from it, in fact.

The things I'd been forced to endure back home... were different. Worse.

Objectified and depersonalized until I was more a *thing* than a person.

Here...they need me in a way that I've never been needed before. Breccan, despite his brash, animalistic nature, has shown me tenderness that I haven't experienced in a long time, if ever. I'm cared for, given blinding orgasms, and made to feel wanted and...needed.

Would I feel like that if I went back home? Had I ever? Here, I'm shocked to realize I feel almost... content. I can't remember the last time I felt content at home without the help of a drug-induced stupor, and even then it was only fleeting.

I know I should still want to leave. I know I have to try to save the other women.

But now...now I'm not so sure if I want to go home at all.

I'm not even sure I want to know what's going on back on my planet. Somehow...some way, I ended up in one of those cryotubes and was jetting through space. Asleep. The idea is terrifying. Especially since I don't remember a thing. Was I kidnapped? Was I forced away? Now that my mind has found some clarity, questions continue to plague me of how I came to get myself in that position anyway. And if someone put me there, why would I be in any hurry to get back?

I wouldn't.

Not living in a constant haze is nice. I'm beginning to want things for myself again. Stirrings of purpose flitter inside of me.

I'm more than Aria Delaney, actress.

Fierce. Resilient. Tough.

I've lived through some daunting trials in life and yet here I am. Stuck on a creepy planet with sexy albino vampire giants with elf ears and it doesn't totally suck. Nope, it doesn't suck at all.

Perhaps the more I get to know these guys, maybe I'll feel more inclined to stay. Maybe I can help them. On my own terms.

Maybe we're not so different after all.

[9]
BRECCAN

AVRELL APPLIES A MEDICATED wipe to the biggest sore on my chest. I let out a roar and puncture the bedding with my claws. "Rekk! Are you trying to burn a hole right through me?"

Aria comes up beside him and regards me with narrowed eyes. "That was reckless." Her nostrils flare and her lips press together in a firm line. It's as though she's chiding me too. "You passed out." She motions at my chest. "And look at you. You damn near cooked!"

"Do I smell rogcow?" Hadrian questions, sniffing loudly as he strolls into the medical bay.

"Calix cleared you, I see," I bark out, changing the subject. "Did the sabrevipe's claws get you?"

Hadrian unzips his minnasuit and peels out of the top half to show me his wounds. His pale white skin has been scratched and bubbles up red but it has not been punctured.

"How big was this thing?" Aria utters, shock in her voice as she inspects Hadrian's marks. Her fingers flit up as though she wants to touch him but she keeps her distance.

"Don't worry," he whispers loud enough for me to hear. "I don't bite...unless you want me to." He waggles his eyebrows and bares his double fangs, causing her to giggle.

Giggle!

That rekking mort gets on my every last nerve most solars now that he's come into his own, but right now I want to hug him and thank him for bringing some genuine joy to my mate.

It strikes me as I watch her appraise his battle wounds and chatter with him that she's not happy. Not happy like I am. She's the best rekking thing to happen to me in my entire existence.

But her?

We essentially took her from somewhere.

My mind throbs with questions. About her family. Her duties. The things she enjoys doing or holds dear to her. I know nothing.

"What is it?" Avrell asks as he listens to my heart

with his device. "Your pulse is thumping erratically. I'm worried you may have some UV poisoning."

"It was bigger than this room!" Hadrian boasts, stretching his arms to describe the baby sabrevipe.

Aria shrieks in horror. "No! And you took it down by yourself?"

"While everyone watched," he agrees. "You're talking to the future commander when my old man kicks it."

She laughs again and my heart thumps in my chest. Avrell panics and rushes over to his medicine cabinet.

"Av," I grunt. "It's not UV poisoning." My eyes trek over to Aria. It's her.

Avrell's gaze follows mine and we watch as Hadrian pretends to run and battle this giant he's made up in his nog.

"You'd make a great actor," she tells him, her giggles echoing in the room.

"I don't know what that is but I do know I'd make a great *everything*." He grins like the empty-nog little rekk he is.

"Go help Galen cook this massive beast that you single-handedly destroyed," I order dryly.

He flashes me his rogcow horns and saunters out of the medical bay like he's the mortarekking king of

Mortuus. Avrell lets out an amused chuckle as he returns without the medicine for UV poisoning but instead an electrolyte booster. I toss the tablet into my mouth and crunch the chalky pill. As soon as I swallow, I can feel my strength returning.

"Why did those monsters attack the facility?" she asks, fear flashing in her brown orbs. "Can they get in? Will they eat us?" She shudders and rubs her arms.

I climb off the table, no longer dizzy, and pull her slight frame into my arms. At first, she is stiff, but then she leans against my chest that is still far warmer than normal. It prides me knowing I can comfort her. Even if it is only to make her stop shivering.

I want to comfort her soul like Hadrian did in a few short moments.

"The morts around here work 'round the clock to keep things out. The beasts, the elements, the pathogens." I stroke her soft hair that I've grown quite fond of touching. "I'll keep you safe. This solar and every solar after, mortania."

Avrell chuckles behind me. "Quite the rogstud, Commander."

Rekking rogstud. A beast that mounts a rogcow to breed little calves. Walks around grunting with his cock always eager and ready. When he's ready to rut on his female, he brays this mortarekking sound that'll make you want to flatten your ears against your skull and pin them there so you don't have to hear it anymore. It's terrible.

I am not a rekking rogstud.

Her nose scrunches as she looks up at me. "Mortania?"

"Means beautiful female," Avrell explains, a smile in his voice.

Grunting, I tug her with me out of the room. "See you later in the nutrition bay," I call over my shoulder.

"Nobody will fault you if you don't show up," he yells out after me. "Try to keep the braying down though. Makes the others jealous."

I glare at him over my shoulder and he flashes me the rekking horns Hadrian is always throwing my way. These morts are all losing their minds. Every last one of them.

"WHY DON'T we eat with the others?" Aria asks as we carry our trays to my quarters.

I swipe my new armband on the reader since I've seemed to have misplaced my other one. Usually Hadrian is the only one who loses his belongings around here. Perhaps I am too distracted by my new alien and behaving like a young mort again. Careless and idiotic.

"Why *would* we eat with them?" I'm perplexed why we would do such a thing. I've seen the way Hadrian eats. Makes a mess all over the place. I don't want to see that while I'm consuming my meal. It'll make your stomach churn.

She walks into my room and sits down at the table —a table that earlier this solar was toppled over when my mate was bored and lonely without me.

Confusing thoughts vie for space in my mind. A part of me knows she is the key to our future. She'll be my mate and produce my young. But the other part of me wonders about the way my mother and father interacted. My mother laughed often. Father was jovial like Hadrian. Perhaps I need to work on making my mate laugh. Then, she will not give me hate eyes while I gift her my seed.

"That's what families do," she says with a huff. She picks up her utensil and pokes at the seared sabrevipe tenderloin on her plate. "They eat together."

Sitting down across from her, I regard my mate. The anger and fear has bled from her features and curiosity dances there. Curiosity is something I'm familiar with and am equipped to deal with. Once, I spent an entire solar describing for Hadrian every beast that lives on the planet.

Every. Single. Beast.

In detail.

"*We* are a family then," I agree as I pick up my tenderloin and bite into it. Succulent juices rush over my tongue and I groan. We haven't had good meat in ages. For many solars, we've been wasting away on Galen's green-bunches. A handful of leafy plants sprinkled with some sauce he came up with. It tastes decent, but I prefer meat. A mort was meant to eat meat. Unfortunately for us, meat is hard to come by.

I've downed everything on my plate, including the small portion of green-bunches which taste especially bitter this solar, when I feel her eyes on me. When I look up, her utensil is still poised in her hand but she hasn't touched anything. Her expression is sad and her delicious tears threaten to leak down her spotted cheeks. Perhaps I'll lick her for an after-dinner sweet.

"I already have a family," she murmurs. Her shoulders slump forward. "Had."

Guilt infects me as I try to imagine this family. "You had a mate?" I ask, my voice husky. I'd not considered this. Hadn't even asked. What if she has a mate from her planet? Worse yet, younglings?

She sniffles. "No. No husband or boyfriend. But I

113

had a mother and father. And my little sister, Limerick."

A sister?

I don't know what to say. My heart aches for her. Our world is so barren and empty. The solars my parents were each taken from me were so trying on my mind. I'd nearly collapsed in on myself. There was no light in my world for a long time. Just solars and solars and solars of nothing but never-ending darkness.

She's suffering the darkness too.

My sweet mate's heart hurts for her family.

Normally, I make decisions and lead my faction without faltering. Yet now, I am unsure what to do. At a loss of what to say.

"Eat," I bite out, harsher than I mean.

She flinches and the sweet tears leak from her eyes. Her eyes drift from mine to the meat on her tray. With her utensil, she stabs at it.

Rekk!

Her useless teeth. I'm an awful mate. She'd be better matched with someone like Hadrian. Someone who makes her laugh. Or maybe Avrell. Tender and concerned about her well-being.

Yet...

She's stuck with me.

Perhaps she didn't destroy our quarters because she missed me.

It was because she detests me.

I must correct her feelings. Make her understand I can learn. It was I who learned, through trial and error, what half the machines in this rekking facility do. Someone had to figure it out and teach the rest.

"Allow me," I utter in a softer tone. I stab the meat with three of my claws and then use my other hand to rip smaller pieces from the tenderloin. I'm careful to make them tiny, like her mouth. "When Hadrian was younger and his double fangs hadn't grown in yet, I used to have to cut up his meat. That empty-nog mort still makes attempts to have me cut up his food." I shake my nog but I can't keep the smile off my face. "He's not my mortling but he may as well be. I've raised him."

When I lift my gaze, her sad expression has melted away and she smiles at me. Rekk, I love her smiles.

"You're like his adoptive dad?"

I don't understand the words but I get the meaning. "I'd die for him if that is what you infer, mortania."

Her cheeks blush at the name Avrell teased me about earlier. I will call her that often. My little alien likes to be told she is beautiful.

"That's sweet," she says, a smile tugging at her lips.

But then she grows serious. "This is all so..." She trails off. "Different." She stabs one of the small niblets of meat with her utensil and takes a bite. Her eyes widen and a groan escapes her. "Oh my God. This is so good. Kevin wouldn't let me have meat. Said I was more sellable as a vegan."

More words I don't understand.

Except Kevin.

I pick up on the distasteful way she said the name.

"Who is Kevin?" I growl, unable to keep the jealous bite out of my tone. So much for being gentle and kind to my mate.

She doesn't flinch this time but instead sits up straight, leveling me with a hard glare. "Kevin is my talent manager. He makes sure my hair and makeup are always on par. Kevin chooses my wardrobe. And Kevin decides on the roles I will take. He owns me." Her throat flashes bright red and she will no longer meet my gaze. "Last year, he started getting me more revealing roles."

I tilt my nog and try to understand her gibberish.

She continues with a heavy sigh. "He was the one to give me my first hit of flora. To 'calm me down.'" She laughs bitterly. "I calmed down all right." More tears spring in her eyes.

My chest hurts from seeing pain practically

bleeding from her. I want to hold her in my arms until it disappears. But something tells me she needs to get this out. Like the time Draven nearly went mad. I had to lock us in a reform cell. He ranted and ranted for three solars straight. With only me to listen. I let him take his rage out on me, much to Avrell's horror. And eventually, when Draven let it all out, he found some peace.

I'll help my little alien find her peace.

This...this is something I can do. Something that Avrell or Hadrian or any other mort here isn't capable of. I am the strongest. I can handle it.

"Tell me more, Aria. If you must unleash the rage on me, I am your willing victim."

She blinks at me and lets out a small laugh. A sweet laugh. *I* made her laugh. Too bad I wasn't trying to be humorous. Small strides though. I will count it as progress.

"You wouldn't understand," she says suddenly, the laughter dying in her throat. Her eyes are cold.

"I will try for you. I can be patient," I assure her. I reach across the table and grasp her hand. She tries to pull away but I don't let her.

"This!" she snarls, her voice cruel. "This is why you won't understand." She whaps my knuckles with her utensil.

I jerk back, my hand smarting in pain. What did I do wrong? My ears flatten against my nog, preparing for battle.

I can't battle my mate though.

Rekk, she is so confusing.

"You're all the same!" she yells, rising from her seat. "Every goddamned planet, you're all the same! Predators!"

We are, in fact, predators, but I don't interrupt her to point out this fact.

"You're just like Kevin," she spits out.

I mimic her movements and stand. "Is he a fine hunter?"

She blinks at me in confusion. "What? No. He eats takeout and has a spray tan. No, he's not a fine hunter."

"Ahh," I say in understanding. "Your Kevin is a fine leader. Strong and cunning."

She mutters out a string of words that make no sense but she seems furious. Her shoulders tremble with anger. I reach forward and hold my hand out to her like she did with Hadrian earlier. Asking to touch but worried of what might happen.

Her brown eyes meet mine and she reaches up to press her palm to my own. "Kevin is nothing to me. He is not a fine leader. But he *is* cunning and strong."

Our fingers thread together and I gently pull her

closer. Much to my surprise, she allows me to pull her into an embrace. I realize I must treat her like a mortling throwing a fit. Hadrian was a mortarekking terror when he was small. But all it would take was me pulling him into my lap and stroking his back to calm him. I run my knuckles along the bones in her back.

She relaxes against me and my heart sings inside its cage like a jackaw bird. They're not much for eating but they're entertaining to watch and listen to when they flit about, chirping songs that fill your soul. Often, when looking out the windows in the command center, I watch the jackaws. One of my few moments of enjoyment.

That is, until my mate arrived.

Now every moment is one that fills me with excitement.

"Kevin abused his power," she murmurs against my still-sore chest. "He abused *me*."

Something in the way she says her words makes my blood grow cold. "This Kevin hurt you?"

She tilts her nog up and frowns at me. "He got me addicted to flora. And when I was flying high, he'd fuck me."

I blink at her in confusion. "What is this fuck?"

"What *we* do, Breccan!" she hollers in exasperation. "What *you* do to me!" Hot tears roll down her cheeks as a sob racks through her. "Let me break this down in a way you can understand. He paralyzed me with his 'toxica,'" she explains, and makes a gesture with two fingers on each hand as though she's clawing the air. "And then...then he stuck his dick inside me. It made me feel sick and dirty and used. He'd try to *breed* with me."

My mind turns black with rage.

This Kevin dares copulate with *my* mate?

I rekking think not!

"I will cut his flesh from his bones and feed it to the biggest sabrevipe on this rekking planet!" I roar, and break away from her. I must destroy something. If I can't have this Kevin, I'll destroy the mortarekking wall.

She watches, unmoving, as I rip a cabinet from the wall and slam it to the ground. I expect her to retreat in fear but my fierce mate stays strong as I throw a tantrum young Hadrian would be proud of, wrecking the room I worked so diligently to clean earlier. It would seem my mate and I both like to break things. A common bond.

"You are mine," I seethe. "He cannot even carry you. He does not know how to hunt. This Kevin is worthless! A piece of radiation-tainted dirt on the bottom of my boot."

Her eyes widen. "You're missing the point, you big evil-looking elf-eared vampire!"

My ears flatten against my nog and I pop all the sub-bones in my neck before baring my double fangs at her. "You are safe here. I will slice open this Kevin if I ever see him."

A smile tugs at her lips. "That's kind of sweet in a psycho kind of way."

"Sweet like your delicious tears and tongue, mortania?"

Her lashes bat against her cheeks and she softens toward me. "You truly don't understand." A heavy sigh escapes her. "Your intentions are pure, I get it. You want to breed and create life on this planet."

I nod with a smile. "Yes."

She purses her lips. "At my expense."

"I want other things too, besides breeding." My cock stiffens. Breeding is definitely on the top of the list. But her smiles are a close second. "I want to make you laugh like Hadrian does." I take a step toward her and raise my hand. Again, she doesn't hesitate and presses her palm to mine. "Aria, I want you to relax in my presence like you do with Avrell." Our fingers link once more. "I want to feed you and care for you. I do not want this takeout and the spray tans you speak of that this useless Kevin desires."

She lets out a snort and then cackles. Just like with Hadrian. I still wasn't trying to be humorous, but I like that I am skilled enough that I don't need to be an empty-nog boaster like my boy to get her to laugh. He has much to learn if he wants to be as competent a commander as myself.

I tug her to my body and she relaxes against me. Perhaps my efforts are working. I stroke her hair, mimicking what my father used to do with my mother. A small purr escapes her. My cock is hard between us, eager to press inside her and fill her with my seed.

"Breccan, I want a choice," she says, her words firm. "Kevin didn't give me a choice. *You* didn't give me a choice. I want to be able to say no and you'll listen."

I lean my bumpy forehead against her smooth one. "You want to choose our breeding times?"

"Essentially, yes."

"If this is your wish, I will grant it, mortania."

She slides her palms up my still smarting in pain chest over my minnasuit. Her fingers run gently through my long black hair and I close my eyes. The feeling brings me the same overwhelming sensations that the UV rays do.

"I just want to kiss for now," she tells me, her voice low and alluring.

"Kiss?"

"Your tongue rubbing against mine." She grins at me. "As long as you don't bite me with those scary teeth of yours."

I understand this, and quite enjoy her sweet taste.

"I will rub your tongue with mine until you beg me to stop, little alien." It appears I will have my after-dinner sweet after all. "Anything to bring you joy. I would never hurt you, not even with my teeth."

She flinches and a moment passes between us because we both know she's been known to use hers before.

"You're not like Kevin at all," she murmurs before standing on her toes and shoving her delicious tongue into my mouth. And as promised, I'm careful as I *kiss* her.

Pride surges through me.

I am *not* like takeout-spray-tan-non-hunting Kevin.

We both seem to like this fact very much.

SCREAMS.

Terrified and sad.

I wake in my darkened room with a start, searching for my frightened alien. My sub-bones crack and pop as I shield her from whatever has her crying out in fear.

"Shhh," I murmur once I realize her nog is filled with bad memories or made up horrors much like Hadrian suffered from as a mortling. No real terrors await her. "You're safe, little alien."

She clings to my chest and pride fills me. I stroke my claws through her hair and press my lips to her nog. When her breathing evens out, I almost fall asleep. But when her tiny fingers flitter over my bare flesh just above the waistband of my trousers, a low groan rumbles through me.

Don't touch her.

It's her choice.

Everything in me begs to push her onto her bed, spread her pink legs apart, and drive into her slick cunt. Instead, I respect her wishes. I ignore my aching hardness pressed between us.

"Kiss me," she whispers, her hot breath tickling my skin.

I tangle my clawed fingers in her hair and tilt her head back. My lips brush along hers. What she calls kissing is the second-best thing to mating. I enjoy it immensely. She parts her mouth and allows my forked tongue to taste her sweetness. I lick her as though I can extract every tasty drop from her mouth. Moans fill the air as she gives in to the way I maul her with my mouth. She playfully bites my bottom lip and I let out a hiss.

"Kiss my neck," she orders.

I'm happy to oblige. She may not want to mate but touching and tasting her doesn't seem off limits. I run my lips along her cheek to her jawline and to her neck. My turn to tease her back. Scraping my sharp double fangs over her flesh, I relish in the way she moans with delight. This little alien likes the promise of danger it would seem. I tongue her flesh that tastes more pungent than her mouth. I crave to lick every part of her.

"Let me taste you, Aria," I beg. I may be the commander around here but I'm as weak as a newborn mortling when it comes to her. I'll take whatever she gives to me.

"Y-Yes," she croaks out. "Down there."

I frown in the dark. I'm not sure what 'down there' means. Sliding my palm over her breast, I whisper, "Here?"

"No."

I slip it further down to where her stomach will hopefully swell one day with my mortling. "Here?"

"No," she breathes. "There."

Moving my palm to her cunt over her pants, I gently touch her. "Here?"

"Yes. Kiss me there."

"Do you want me to remove these?" I ask as I tug at the fabric.

"Yes," she says, a smile in her voice, "because I want you kiss me with your tongue."

A growl rumbles through me but I force myself to be calm and remove her clothing without ripping it from her body. Once I've bared her naked flesh to me, I push her knee to the side. Her scent is musky and makes my mouth water. Leaning forward, I press my lips to neck once more before I start tonguing my way down her body. She makes a whimpering sound that has my cock seeping with my seed.

"You smell unlike anything I've ever scented," I murmur as I reach her small tuft of hair between her thighs. "Perfection, little alien."

She cries out when I slide my long tongue between her lower lips of her cunt. The taste is a nectar of The Eternals. More delicious than anything I've ever feasted on. I become ravenous as I practically eat my alien. The urge to bite her is intense but something tells me she wouldn't like it. Her juices become more fluid and slide over my tongue, dizzying me. I become engrossed in my task. *Kissing* her cunt. Each mewl and whimper spurs me on.

"Let me kiss you inside, Aria," I rumble against her

sweet flesh. "Let me put my tongue inside you. You may not want my cock but let me taste you. I beg of you, sweet alien."

Her fingers tangle in my mane and she yanks me closer. "Yes. Just your tongue. I want it."

I groan and begin sliding it into her tight hole that's meant for my cock. My tongue disagrees though as I explore her deeply. Sounds rattling from her are ragged and uneven. Desperate. Curling my tongue up, I'm delighted to find something within her that makes her cry out in pleasure.

"Breccan!"

I love how she says my name and I rub at the small nodule within her. It fits perfectly in the groove between the two tines of my tongue. She jolts and spasms, her juices running freely from her the tastiest flavor my mouth has ever known. My nose is pressed against her pleasure button. I decide I want to pleasure her there as well. Moving back and forth, I use my nose to rub against the throbbing flesh while my tongue teases her within.

I like kissing inside her.

I like it very much.

"Breccan!" she screams loud enough to wake the entire facility.

Before I can shush her, she comes violently. Her

body thrashes and she gifts me with more of her sweet nectar. I don't stop sucking and licking and tasting until she pushes me forcefully away.

"Enough," she breathes. "No more. Please."

For a moment, I worry I've hurt her. I wrap my arms around her thin thighs and rest my cheek against her cunt.

"I am sorry, little alien."

Her fingers gently caress through my hair. "Don't be sorry for that. Not ever. That," she says with a soft sigh. "That was everything."

She soon falls asleep and my lids grow heavy. I must get my rest if I plan on kissing her cunt when she wakes.

And I will be kissing her there over and over again until she begs me to stop.

That was everything.

I can't wait to give her everything every solar.

[10]
ARIA

"WHAT DO you mean I'm doing it wrong?" I glance down at the pieces of scrap metal scattered over my lap. I've been working on helping Ozias repair the alien version of a tablet. I have no idea what I'm doing, but I've made it a point not to stay cloistered in Breccan's room, avoiding everyone. In truth, I'm trying to stay busy so I don't think about sex, and if that means I have to pretend to know what I'm doing, then so be it.

Ozias—or Oz, as Jareth calls him—merely smiles and reaches across the table between us to join two wires together, causing the tablet to chirp to life. Oz is the tinkerer of the group. Despite the fact his hands are always smeared with grease and his pockets filled with scraps of paper and spare parts, his clothes and hair are always impeccable otherwise. Unlike his good buddy Jareth, Oz is quieter one. It makes it all too easy for me to ramble when I'm in his presence.

My eyes widen and I smile back at him. "Thank you! I hope you realize I have no idea what I'm doing here. I don't even know why you're letting me help you. I'm doing more damage than help at this point, I think."

His fingers move quickly as he rewires his own tablet. I try to follow along, but he's simply too quick for my human eyes to track. "I enjoy the company, little one. It's been just us morts for far too long."

I continue trying to tinker with the tablet. It's been three days—solars, they call them—since Breccan took me to the command center and received those horrible UV burns. Three days since I'd admitted my secret to him. Three days without any pressure to breed for them. But even though we're not having sex, he's gladly gone down on me each night.

That tongue.

I could almost orgasm thinking about it.

Horror washes over me as I wonder if Oz can smell my arousal. His brows are furrowed in concentration so I'm hoping not. Forcing my thoughts elsewhere, I think about how my days have been spent because it's a much safer topic than my nights.

I've explored the facility with free rein. I couldn't

quite bring myself to use the armband to access the other girls in cryo, not yet. They were safe and so was I —for now. Best for me to learn as much about the facility as I could while I had the opportunity.

So far, in addition to tagging along with Oz, I've spent time with Avrell in the medical bay, treating sprains and wounds of the various inhabitants. By far the most frequent patient is the dark and broody Draven, who I have yet to gather the courage to approach alone. Breccan mentioned he's a little crazy, so I've kept my distance. The other morts have spoken to me in passing, but most are too bamboozled by my presence to maintain a conversation. They may be intimidating in stature and appearance, but underneath, I'm learning they're really quite...human.

"How long?" I ask after a few moments of companionable silence.

"Pardon me?"

"How long has it been just the ten of you living in this place?"

The outside world—The Graveyard, as they call it —is a dangerous place with countless ways to suffer a painful death. The radiation and sabrevipes are just the start.

For the first time, Oz pauses his tinkering and his eyes flick to me. His ears lie flat and his eyes turn to narrow slits, in an action I've come to learn means they're on the offensive, preparing to attack or are experiencing extreme emotion. Then, a few seconds later, his muscles unclench and he relaxes. After a long, fraught pause, he says, "It's been so many revolutions, I've lost count. Before you arrived, we'd lost hope. For a long time, we were preparing to greet death. Breccan—" He breaks off with a sharp look at me.

I'd be kidding myself if I said I wasn't interested. "Breccan what?"

"There's a contingency plan in place if we are ever overcome by another disease like the one that wiped out our people."

"Contingency plan? And what does this have to do with Breccan?" Despite myself, my pulse quickens in my throat. Knowing Breccan, it can't be good, or rather, it'll be something that'll make me want to throttle him.

"You shouldn't worry yourself. Now that you and the other little aliens are here, we have nothing to worry about. Avrell is as good with medicine as I am with machines. They'll have you pregnant with little mortlings in no time and all will be well."

I hold my tongue against explaining that any mortlings have been put on hold. I can't steal the hopeful gleam in his eye, not when we've gotten along so well all morning. Aside from Hadrian and Avrell, Oz is the only other mort I've been able to have a conversation with.

"What about Breccan, Oz? As the future mother of his children, I have a right to know."

He sets the tablet aside and scratches at his thick, long hair. It's even longer than mine, and if I'm being completely honest, I'm a little jealous of how it falls in inky black waves down his muscular shoulders. "When The Rades struck, our numbers suffered greatly. We did everything we could to save who we could, but many lives were lost. Nearly all of them. We're still unsure if we're susceptible to contracting it out there beyond the facility. It's a risk and a constant worry."

"That explains your obsession with germs and cleanliness."

"Exactly, little one." He beams at me like a proud older brother, and his affection and pride warm my heart. "When we were able to regroup, Breccan, as our leader, thought it important to create a plan in case we were ever struck by the disease again. We argued with him for many solars, but he wouldn't be swayed."

My guts churn, and I don't think it's from the

strange grains they served me for breakfast. "What does he want to do?"

Oz, no longer able to stay in one place, moves around the mechanical wing he shares with Jareth and Theron. "You must understand the disease...it's terribly painful for those who contract it. Blistering wounds. Phantom pains. Delirium. It's also highly contagious. No one caught The Rades when Draven did which is by miracle—one that Avrell and Calix were both baffled by. It is assumed though that if one of us were to fall ill, it's all but certain we all would. We can't hope for another pardon like with Draven. As the commander, Breccan will take it upon himself to limit our suffering, if it comes to that."

Had they opened a hatch? Because it seems like all the air has been sucked from the room. "Limit your suffering?" I repeat. "What does that mean?"

"It means, little one, that if we get sick again, Breccan will send us to The Eternals and then take his own life. No mort wants to live alone. It's bad enough being forced to live without a mate—to a mort, that's as close to death as one can be. But for one of us to live alone for the rest of our life, it would be a fate worse than death."

His revelation stuns me to silence as he continues to work on another stack of tablets.

If I don't stay, if I use the armband to free the other women and escape, isn't that what I'll be condemning these morts to—a fate worse than death? Without me and the children I can potentially provide, they'll die off one by one in this lonely, isolated facility on a planet even more dangerous and depressing than my own.

How can I leave them here when I have the ability to save them?

I try, fruitlessly, to replicate Oz's steps to repair the tablet, but after an hour or so more of his patient instruction, I'm no further along than I was when I started. My mind is too preoccupied with my dilemma to focus on the wires and circuits.

Breccan comes to collect me after his rounds. I look up from the tablet and find him posed in the doorway, watching me with his version of a smile. It's too fierce to be classified as such and if pressed, I'd call it more of a grimace.

A wave of affection washes over me, for this big, strange alien I've come to view as my own. The kind of man who'd make the hard decisions to save his people from the task. Who'd be strong enough to see them through, and he would, I know he would.

Those big, onyx eyes study me hungrily and I shiver. The newfound intimacy inspired by our conversation about Kevin and his endless patience since undoes me. But it's the total realization that he is willing to die for his men that rocks me to the core. It makes me realize, truly, the life I've squandered in my own world. The days I'd given up to drugs and delirium. My sister, my only decent family, I'd been willing to blow off with drugs.

Whereas Breccan, sweet Breccan, is prepared and ready to do much worse for his men. These gruff beings know more about how precious life is than I can even begin to understand. But it isn't just about the babies, though I'm coming to learn how important family—and mates—are to them, but also about how they cherish each moment. The world here is so harsh, so unpredictable, they have to suck the marrow out of every day because they aren't promised another.

My heart races in anticipation. I don't want to waste another day, another one of those precious moments. I want to live, as they do, with joy for every second I'm alive.

I want to enjoy it all...with Breccan.

The thought steals my breath.

"Time for a break," he commands, "before this one has you tinkering at all hours of the solar like he does."

"I'm afraid your mate has no aptitude for repair work, Commander."

Their conversation filters through the buzzing in my ears. I can barely catch a breath to respond. "Be nice, Oz."

Breccan strides forward and wraps an arm around my waist. He nips at my lips with his sharp fangs, which causes me to shiver against his warmth. As he nuzzles my neck, he whispers, "You've spent far too long away from me, my Aria."

My fingers dig into his minnasuit as my body sings in agreement. The time he's given me to get to know each other without the pressure of sex has left me... wanting. Wanting him. To kiss, to take. I can't help but soften against him—and *toward* him. The nights spent *kissing* are a tease that leaves me aching for more than just his tongue inside me.

"It's only been a couple hours," I protest, but my body doesn't—and I lean into him.

"As I said, much too long. Ozias has been monopolizing your time."

Oz takes no offense. "I'm happy to entertain her anytime you like, Brec. I much prefer her company to yours."

I drag Breccan away before they butt heads—literally. It wouldn't be the first time I came across a pair of quarreling morts settling their differences by battling it out like a couple of animals. I have no interest in seeing

Breccan doing so. I'm much more interested in kissing. I can barely keep my hands off him as we trek back to his quarters.

"Is something the matter, my alien?" he asks when I push him up against a wall in the corridor and attack his throat. He bares it for me, and there's something powerful in the knowledge that this big, strong alien is willing to be vulnerable for the sake of my pleasure. A growl reverberates in his chest as I suck and bite at his pale white skin. I can't get enough of the satin-like texture. All I can think about is feeling it rub against my skin with no suit, no clothing between us.

I try to reach his mouth, but he's too tall for me. I grab his ears instead and tug to bring his lips to mine. "Kiss me," I say instead of answering.

I'm not sure I could put my feelings into words if I tried. His compassion when he listened to my struggles about my talent manager, his willingness to give me time to come to terms with my decision, his sacrifice for his men. I've never encountered a better man than him. Sometime between waking up on this lost planet and now, I've softened for the big guy. It doesn't hurt that he's grown to be a phenomenal kisser in the short time we've been "practicing".

"Would you like me to kiss you elsewhere?" he taunts playfully.

A needy groan escapes me. "Take me to bed, Breccan," I say against his lips. "I want to do more than kiss. I don't want to think about anything. I don't want to worry about either of our fates. I want you to make me forget everything. I just want it to be me and you. Like we met somewhere and hit it off and you took me home. Can it just be me and you and nothing else?"

His clawed hands rake back my hair and then he cups my cheek. "I don't understand your urgency, mortania, but I will do whatever you need. I'm here to ease all your fears, and I want nothing more than to lie with you."

He picks me up then, and sprints to the room, his long, powerful legs traveling one step for what would have been three of mine. I hang on for dear life and pray I'm not making a mistake.

Then I decide, to hell with it.

I deserve one night to have him without reservation.

After that, I'll decide what I'm going to do.

But for now, I plan to lose myself in my mate—because it may be the only chance I get.

[11]
BRECCAN

HER BROWN EYES gleam with hunger. More intense and fierce than the look half my morts had when we had to live forty-seven solars straight on Galen's green-bunches alone. But I don't think she's hungry for sustenance.

She's hungry for me.

I think about the way she bit my throat with her useless teeth. My cock stiffens. Little Aria can attempt to feed on me all she wants as long as she lets me stick my tongue in her sweet mouth. Her kissing is one of my favorite things. I don't think she realizes she tastes so rekking good. I lose my mind on her taste alone. So much so, that I find myself craving her more than the UVs. I'm completely healed and haven't been back since.

I'm stronger because of her.

The darkness that lives inside is being chased away by her light.

With each smile and word, she changes me.

Her eyes remain on mine as she begins undressing. Her body is pink and soft. The swells of her breasts seem to speak a language only my cock knows. I let my eyes trail down to her tuft of brown hair. I'm quite fond of the way it tickles my nose when I lick her cunt.

"Take your clothes off," she demands, her voice fierce. She is a fine mate for a commander.

"At your service, Madam Commander."

She laughs. And, rekk, I *was* trying to be humorous this time. Our moments together are becoming easier and I think we are learning a lot about each other. I'm certainly learning how to make her smile more. I count them and store them away in my mind to get me through dark thoughts. Horrible memories of my past or a future without her in it. Sometimes the blackness eats at my mind. She chases it away though.

I peel away my minnasuit and am undressed within seconds. I abandon my boots and suit to prowl her way. My cock bobs, eager to have her, but I've grown wise to Aria's ways. Stopping before our chests touch, I look down at her and stroke my claws through her silky hair.

She runs her fingertips down my chest and my cock jumps, tapping her soft body. Her eyes narrow as she slides her hand between us and grips it. "He's happy to see me," she purrs.

"You speak of him as if he has his own mind," I growl. "*I'm* happy to see you."

Her smile is my undoing. She gently strokes my shaft. "I'm happy to see you too. All of you." She bites on her bottom lip that I want to bite too. "I missed being with you." She turns and points at the bed. "Lie down, lover boy."

Amused by her bossy behavior, I obey my mate and stretch out on the bed, my cock pointing straight up. She walks over to me, her breasts bouncing with her movement. When she's filled with my child, her breasts will swell with sustenance for our mortling. That's something I do remember from my past.

"We are to mate like this?" I ask with a raised brow.

She tosses her hair over her shoulder as she straddles me. "We are. Do you have a problem with that, Commander?"

"And when my toxica hits your system? What will happen then?" I tease.

Her hand wraps around my cock again and she eases herself over my tip. "You'll catch me if I fall."

143

We both groan when she sinks all the way down, my cock filling her to capacity.

"I'll always catch you," I vow, my teeth gritting in pleasure.

She rests her palms on my chest and begins rocking her hips in a way that makes me want to flip her and thrust into her hard. But the satisfied smirk on her face has me fisting the bedsheets instead, allowing her this control she so adamantly craves.

"You feel so good," she murmurs.

"You do too, my mate."

Her nog falls back and she rubs at her breasts as she does all the work.

"Allow me to assist," I growl as I pluck one of her palms from her breast and replace it with mine. I mimic the way she was rubbing her thumb over her nipple and gently scrape my claw over the peaked flesh. She cries out and her cunt clenches around my cock.

"Breccan," she moans, her body shaking with impending pleasure. "Touch me here, too." Her free hand grabs my wrist and guides me between her lower lips. Careful to retract my claw, I massage her there as well.

"You like mating with me," I observe, my voice hoarse.

"I do," she agrees. "So much."

"You like being the commander in bed." I pinch her nipple between two of my claws, pulling her closer to me. "Will you allow me to taste your sweet tongue, Madam Commander?"

She moans and nods, her movements becoming frantic as she seeks my mouth with hers. Pleasure is zinging through my every nerve ending. I could do this with my little alien every second of every solar. I should promote Hadrian and spend the rest of my existence doing exactly this. I'd die a happy mort.

Her weak teeth bite my bottom lip before she spears her tongue back inside my mouth. I'm impressed at the way she moves her hips. As though she knows exactly what will feel good to me. Wise and clever, this one.

"I'm going to fill you up with my seed," I warn. "Soon. Are you ready to let me take care of you?"

"Not yet," she whimpers. "So close."

I rub her quickly between her thighs. "Lose yourself, mortania. I will catch you."

She stiffens and cries out, her cunt squeezing me. I can tell she's found her release and it allows me to do the same. A loud, claiming growl rips from me as my cock pumps into her. My seed will take one solar, I'm sure of it. Our bodies worked together this time. I realize now that the times before were incomplete in comparison.

Right now, we may as well be one.

Her body relaxes, the toxica taking effect, and I am ready to collect her just as I promised. I slide her off my emptied cock and pull her against my chest. Stroking her hair, I whisper how beautiful and strong and clever she is. Tears—tears I'd love to lick—soak my chest, but this time they don't feel sad.

And just as promised, the toxica isn't as paralyzing as the time before. She's able to move her hand and lifts it just barely. Knowing what she seeks, I slide my own beneath hers. Her fingers curl in between mine, linking us together.

"Rest, my little alien. I have you now."

I have you forever.

"There's no knobs or levers," she whines as she slaps at the wall of the cleansing tube. "Worst shower ever."

I chuckle and reach past her to push in one of the panels. Warmed water blasts from the ceiling earning a high-pitched screech from my alien. She attempts to burrow her nog against my naked chest to hide from the powerful spray.

"You guys take cleaning so freaking seriously!" She tilts her head up to look at me, pouting. It makes her plump lips more tempting than usual. "I wish I had a bath tub," she muses aloud. Her body keeps rubbing against mine and I'm having trouble staying focused on cleansing us.

"What's a bath tub?" I ask huskily. My cock is throbbing between us.

She grips my aching length and bites on her bottom lip. "You fill it with hot water and soak. It gives you more time to *play*." Her brown eyes darken wickedly and her cheeks turn slightly pink.

"We have plenty of time to play," I say, my palms finding her round rump and squeezing.

"It's not the same," she grumbles but slides her hands to the back of my neck. She gets the soft look in her eyes that pleads for me to take her. I could never deny my sweet alien a thing. "It's more relaxing."

Lifting her, I press her back to the wall and position my cock against her opening. "Close your eyes, Aria. Relax. I'll do all the work so you won't fuss over not having this bath tub."

She grumbles but it turns into a moan as I slide her down my length until she's fully seated. With the water soaking us, she's more slippery and everywhere we rub against each other feels incredible. My mouth seeks hers and I kiss her while I mate with her. It would seem my tongue is made to actively explore her mouth. It belongs there.

I retract my claws and seek out her pleasure button —her clit as she calls it—and rub her until her cunt is clenching around me. Her nog bangs against the panel behind her but she seems to enjoy every panel of my ministrations. Soon, I'm groaning and filling her with my seed. The toxica hits her system, rendering her useless. I hold my little alien, murmuring gentle words to her, until her body begins to move again. Once we've both settled from our pleasure and she's no longer dead weight in my arms, I pull away slightly to look at her.

"I can get used to these showers as long as you're in them with me," she murmurs, a smile tilting her lips on one side.

I lift my fingers to her face and run my fingertips along her soft flesh of her cheek. Normally, I keep my claws out all the time because they're a useful tool. But with my little alien, I enjoy touching her tenderly.

"Tell me something no one else knows about you," she whispers. "Anything, no matter how small."

It takes me a moment to think and while I do, I

wash her. When I finally think of something, I stroke my fingers through her messy wet hair and smile.

"I like jackaws."

"Jackaws?"

"They fly around near the windows and sing. It's beautiful." I purse my lips and blow, mimicking the sound they make.

She lets out a content sigh and then her voice does something more beautiful than any jackaw. The sound is similar to theirs but it's accompanied with words. I stare at her, enraptured. Each word that rings from her fills me to the brim. I don't want her to stop. Eventually, she does, but the bright smile is worth it.

"Singing acapella was one of my talents. Several chick flicks I was cast in called for it. I didn't realize how much I missed singing." Her eyes become glassy with tears. The good kind. My heart sings, too.

"I don't know what any of what you said means. My translator unit is worthless," I grumble but not angrily.

She giggles. "Maybe I should sing some more. I liked the expression on your face."

"You better do it again," I say with a grin. "Just to be sure."

It's been seven solars since Aria took me to bed on her own terms. I'm realizing that it's better that way. Pleasurable for the both of us. She now laughs freely with me and there is a bounce in her step. I love how fond she is of Oz and Avrell and Hadrian. I've even seen Draven smile a time or two, which is unheard of.

Aria is life.

Like a little seedling in Galen's lab.

She grows and grows each solar, and all we can do is watch her in wonder.

Soon, it is my hope, she will bear my young.

Until then, I want to do something special for her. She babbles a lot now and tells me about such things called movies. Her favorites are what she deems "classics". I listen and take notes. I'm unable to remember the names of them all, but I do pay attention to what the heroes of her tales do for their heroines. It feels silly, but the giddiness in her voice as she retells the stories assures me that she won't see me as silly if I replicate them.

And that is exactly what I am doing.

Replicating them.

I've chosen the parts that light her eyes up the most and created a plan. Much like a mission into The Graveyard that must be executed properly and requires the assistance of all my morts, I throw every ounce of energy into pulling off the most successful mission I can.

Hadrian calls it: *Operation Rogstud.*

He can call it whatever the rekk he wants, but all I care about is making her happy.

"Try this," Galen says as he offers me a hard, smooth yellow stone.

"It doesn't seem appealing," I grunt.

Nevertheless, I pop the "candy" into my mouth. Sweetness bursts onto my tongue and I widen my eyes. "It is good." My mate will be pleased.

He grins, baring his double fangs at me. "Well, when Aria started describing the sugary sweet she called butterscotch, it reminded me of a root I came across. The goldenroot has a rich, smooth flavor. I've yet to find a use for it for us, but it's high in vitamins. When she's carrying your young, it will benefit the young one's growth and development."

"I shall feed them to her every second of every solar," I vow.

He laughs. "I've only made twelve. I didn't want to make too many in case they weren't to her liking. The little alien has different tastes than we do. I wanted to be sure."

His pride in helping make my mate happy warms me. I owe him for this. "Thank you, Galen. I'll take the rest as a gift for her. I will make sure she knows of the hard work you put into them for her, and the nutritional value."

With a bounce in his step, he flits around his laboratory collecting things. He's made a soft leathery pouch that's adorned with a black braided drawstring woven into the top. The strands of silver tell me the braid came from his own nog. What a thoughtful gift.

I graciously accept the offering of goldenroot candies and give him a nod before heading out. Hadrian makes a loud racket in the nutrition bay as he works to prepare a meal for Aria and me. All of my morts have their various tasks, and I am grateful. My next step is to visit Calix.

I find him in his lab scratching at the back of his nog as he stares at what he's working on. My chest squeezes as I enter. "Is that it?" I ask in astonishment.

He turns to me, his eyes in offensive slits for a moment before they return to normal. I can see that he is on edge, and I feel guilty for tasking him with something so difficult.

"It's not right, I don't think," he complains.

I walk up to it and run my fingers over the material. "It's almost as though she's standing right before me," I marvel. "The shape of her breasts..." I trail off when a low growl rumbles through me. "How do you know the shape of them?"

His ears flatten against his skull and his eyes return to slits. "I did not touch your mate."

"You just stared at her long enough to memorize her shape?" I hiss.

"I do not want *your* mate," he snarls back. It's almost as though he has more to say. He refrains though. "There is another in the cryochamber who is about her size and shape. I took the measurements from the records there." He turns back to the outfit he has sewn together. "Perhaps I will make more for when the others wake."

It does not bother me that he measured the other aliens.

It would bother me if he touched *my* alien.

"I hope she will love it," I say, my voice calm again.

"It's the same material as our minnasuits. The things she runs around in each solar are not conducive to warding off unwanted bacteria. With this new suit, I will feel safer that she's not a walking, talking, disease-carrying female."

I snort in amusement as he carefully unbuttons the back. Once he's removed the suit from its hanger, he hands it to me. I'm pleased that it will allow me to see the outline of her curves at any time during a solar.

The others will see her curves too but that is something I must live with. They know it is forbidden to even think about touching what's mine.

Once I bid him goodbye, I make my way down to Oz's, where I know she'll be working. I find her inside but instead of working, she's showing him more of her "dancing", as she calls it. Oz is a quick learner and a patient teacher. I'm grateful for him.

"Madam Commander," I tease, making my presence known.

Her brown eyes lift to mine and the smile on her pretty face falls. It is not from sadness, though. Longing glimmers in her gaze. She missed me. I sure as rekk missed her too.

"Time to eat?" she asks as she walks over to me.

I gather her tiny body into my arms and press my lips to hers. Sometimes she prefers her kisses with no tongue. At first, I was adamant we keep the tongue as part of our routine, but then I learned that she likes to do the no-tongue kisses when she is being playful or feels content. Often, the kisses with tongue lead to her bare and spread before me.

I most certainly prefer the tongue kisses.

"What's this?" she asks.

Grinning, I pull away from her to hand her the

new suit. "I had a suit made for you. This solar, I am giving you a date."

She blinks at me and then her eyes become glossy with tears.

At first, I am worried she loathes the idea and maybe I misunderstood everything she spoke of. I glance at Oz and he seems equally upset. We've all worked so hard.

But then she throws herself at me and kisses me with her sweet, delicious tongue. I'm growling and ripping holes in her useless clothing with my claws when she pulls away.

"Thank you for the dress," she says. "I hope it fits. It's so beautiful."

Dress.

Ahh, that is what she calls them.

"Calix made it for you."

Meant to be worn indoors only, he reminded me. Just as she described them to me before, this dress is meant to just look pretty. If she were ever to leave the facility—which she rekking won't—she'd need a proper minnasuit and zu-gear over that.

Her bottom lip wobbles. "That is so sweet. Let me try it on." She rushes into a closet. While we wait for her, Oz brings me the box he had stowed away. I graciously accept it and wait for her to come back out.

"I don't know," she calls out from behind the door. "It's awfully daring."

My heart aches. "You do not like it, my mate?"

"Oh, I love it," she says. "It's so regal. But..."

"Come," I insist, my impatience making it come out like a barked order.

The door creaks open and she steps forward.

Oz makes a choking sound, and I can't take my eyes off her. The midnight-blue material of the minna-suit fits her like a second skin. Just past her hips, the material flares out rather than fitting on her legs. Her small feet are hidden.

She laughs, and her breasts that are pushed up, looking quite tempting as they threaten to spill from the top, quiver with her movements. I'm rekking mesmerized. Oz sounds like he's struggling to breathe.

"I take it you like it?" she says and preens. Playfully, she spins around in a circle and the material magically swishes around her.

"Mortania, you are the best thing my eyes have ever seen," I utter, my voice husky.

"I second that," Oz agrees.

I shoot him a sharp look that has him backing away a step. My ears flatten against my skull and I bare my fangs.

"Cool it, buddy," she sasses as she makes it over to me. "I only have eyes for one male here."

I grip her hip and then run my palm over the material along her ribs. "Mine," I growl.

She laughs again, the sound the happiest I've ever heard her. "Yours. You're such a caveman."

"I'm ready for this date, and then I want to peel this suit from your body, little alien. I want to lick every inch of you, especially between your thighs—"

"Breccan!" She looks over at Oz, who wears a sheepish grin. "We have company."

I want to growl and rage at him to get the rekk out of here but he's helped me so much. Honoring his hard work, I hold out my palm to her. "Jareth and Oz made this for you."

She takes the pieces of flattened zuta-metal that clink together and strung on a thin rope, and holds it up. "They made me a necklace?"

Oz saunters over to us, pride in his every step. "Yes," he agrees. "As you will see, we pounded out the shiniest zuta-metal we own. Breccan mentioned the 'jewelry' you were so fond of. We worked hard to imitate the design. I hope you'll find it to your liking."

She pulls away from me to hug him. I want to drag her back into my arms but I know my little alien hates when I "get all crazy", as she says. She's softer to me if I let her make her own decisions. And right now, she is deciding to hug Oz. A friendly hug, I might add. When we hug, she likes to grab my bottom and squeeze.

"Thank you," she breathes. "Will you help me put it on?"

He beams, his double fangs on full display, as though she has gifted him the highest honor. I watch in amusement as he ties it around her neck. The biggest piece of zuta-metal hangs down and hides the line her breasts have created by being squeezed together. I decide that I like this zuta-metal necklace because my morts won't see a part of her that I am desperate to lick.

She turns to show him, and he smiles so hard I wonder if it hurts. My sweet little alien is so good for my men. One solar soon, I will make sure they have their own aliens. In due time. I'm hesitant to wake them because we still don't know enough about them. Not to mention, there isn't enough to go around. And choosing happiness for one while denying another isn't on my high list of things I'm eager to do.

"It's time," I tell her and hold out my hand.

She grasps it and links our fingers together. When it's quiet and we're alone, this is one of her favorite things to do. I like the way her pink fingers look beside my pale white ones. How we fit together in some unique way.

"This is too kind," she says as we walk down the corridor. "I'm just so happy."

I puff out my chest and grin. "That was the intention. That is my intention with everything I do...to make you happy."

I guide her to the nutrition bay. Hadrian, just as I asked, dragged my table from my room and put it in the middle of this room. I pull out her chair and help her to sit—just like the men from her movies. She lets out a pleased sigh that fills me with hope.

Hadrian, from somewhere hidden, kills the lights. The small dome on the table lights up. I'm not sure if this is close to her candlelight dinner but by the teary way she runs her fingers over the dome and sniffles, I feel as though maybe it does invoke some memories from home. My chest is tight with anxiety but so far, she has loved every one of my gestures.

Hadrian appears, carrying two plates of food. He places them down in front of each of us.

"Rekk," he curses, his eyes glued to my mate's chest.

I growl, causing Aria to giggle. Her breasts jiggle and earn more of Hadrian's attention.

"Uh, that's a nice...zuta-metal mess on your neck,"

he says, attempting to save himself from a throttling.

"Oh, Hadrian," she says in amusement, "it's a necklace. And thank you."

"I've cut your sabrevipe into tiny pieces," he boasts. "And your green-bunches are the greenest, which means they aren't as bitter. Should I cut those up for you too?"

"This is perfect, Hadrian. I can manage."

He nods and scurries off. She smiles and blushes under my intense stare. I don't want to eat. I simply want to look at her. When she realizes I'm not eating, she picks up a piece of her meat with her fingers and holds it up to me.

My mouth waters to taste her more than the meat, so I pounce on the opportunity. I clutch her wrist and draw it closer. Tugging the meat from her grip, I quickly eat it and then dart my forked tongue out. Her breath hitches as I lick the remnants of the meat from her flesh.

"Wow, uh, it's warm in here," she murmurs.

We continue our meal and she tells me all about waterfalls and islands. I don't know about these things but the way she describes them sounds lovely. If I could give them to her, I would. Eventually, we finish and I guide her to the command center, which has been set up for more of our date.

Inside, we find one of the computer screens on. I help her settle into one of the seats and start the recording. This was the trickiest thing, and I have no idea how it turned out. I'm hoping Hadrian didn't make a mess of things.

When it starts, she gasps.

And then laughs.

Laughs and laughs and laughs.

I laugh too.

That mortarekker did not disappoint, and how he managed to rope Draven into it, I haven't a clue. They made her a movie. They're all in it. Galen, Avrell, Calix, Draven, Oz, Jareth, Sayer, Theron, and finally Hadrian.

Acting.

Each male plays himself except Hadrian and Draven. Draven is me, and I must admit his growling is on par with the way I do it. I'm impressed at how tough he looks as he struts along.

But Hadrian? Hadrian is pretending to be Aria. I'm laughing so hard, tears leak from my eyes. Aria is still laughing too.

"Oh, beast, show me your naked cock again you giant rogstud," Hadrian says, his voice high-pitched. He flits around making a fool of himself.

Draven growls. Again. And throws Hadrian over

his shoulder. "Alien, I'm taking you to my lair to put my seed in you over and over again until you're fat with my young." He slaps Hadrian's bottom, and he screeches.

"Not so hard, you mortarekker!"

Draven beams at the source of the recording as he walks around the facility "working" with a squirming Hadrian pretending to be Aria thrown over his shoulder. They even mimic a hunt, where Hadrian whispers loudly for Draven to set him down. Then he's back to being Hadrian, and he kills the "biggest sabrevipe in all the land." Once he struts around, showing his muscles, he dances off the screen and then returns, pretending to be Aria again.

"Hadrian, you're so brave. When the old man kicks it, I'll take you as mine. You can put your seed in me and—"

Draven whaps him in the nog. "Don't disrespect the commander."

"I mean," Hadrian backtracks in his high Aria voice, "I'll be so distraught over the handsome commander that I'll never crawl out of my bed again."

Draven nods, pleased. "'Tis a good thing I am still alive." He starts to unzip his minnasuit—but then he waggles his finger at us. "To see more, you'll have to catch the next one," he says.

All of the morts take a bow and the recording ends.

"Oh my God," Aria giggles through her tears. "You really do pay attention to everything I say." When she settles from her laughter, she stands from her chair and crawls into my lap. "I don't know what could make this date any better aside from the happy ending we'll get later."

I stroke my fingers through her hair. "Candy?"

She moans. "Don't even tease me like that."

With a grin, I pull the pouch from my pocket and hand it to her. Her wide eyes twinkle with excitement as she hurries to open it. The scent permeates the air and she gasps.

"Butterscotch?"

"Not exactly," I say. "They're goldenroot candies. Galen hopes they are to your satisfaction."

She plucks one from the bag and sticks it on her tongue. Her eyes flutter closed and she moans. The good kind of moan. When she reopens her eyes, a foreign emotion swims in them.

"Breccan?"

"Yes, Madam Commander?"

"You did well. Very well." She smiles. "I want a kiss." Her eyes darken and she straddles my lap, where my aching cock is hard beneath her. "With tongue."

[12]
ARIA

I still haven't told Breccan I have his armband.

I know I should, but I can't keep from thinking I may need it at some point. Besides, he got a new one anyway, so it's not like he misses it. Life with the morts has been...indescribable. In my roles back home, I used to act out the happy family, but here...here I'm starting to actually *feel* it. It's a feeling I don't want to lose, and I know if I were to tell him I stole the armband, and have been holding onto my little backup plan, it would destroy that happiness.

We lie in bed, my body still frozen in the aftereffects of the toxica, a few mornings after the unbelievable date they'd planned for me. The paralyzing effects aren't as strong as they used to be, and I've also come to enjoy the way they prolong and enhance my pleasure. It was an aspect I hadn't considered the first time it happened, that giving into it, trusting him to take care of me, would heighten the sensations and draw them out.

"What consumes your thoughts, my mate?" Breccan asks as his claws rake patterns down my bare back.

I smile against his chest, feeling more content than I've ever been in my life despite my worries. "I'm happy."

His claws retract and the smoothness of his fingertips replaces them. He cups the cheeks of my ass and spreads my legs over his hips. I can feel the pleasant thrust of his cock between my thighs and it makes me sigh.

"This brings me pleasure. All I want is to make you happy."

"And what would make *you* happy, Breccan?" He presses me more firmly against the growing hardness between us. "Besides that," I say, but my voice is practically a purr. It should be against the law how skilled these aliens are at lovemaking. Well, my alien anyway.

"You are all I need to be happy."

I blurt the next words, unaware they were even a fear until they spill from my lips. "What if I never get pregnant?"

We've been having sex pretty much daily since I woke up, except for a few days when he was "courting" me. The worry is plain on Avrell's face each time he does a scan and informs me again and again that I'm not pregnant. Breccan, however, has been stoic, resolute. If he worries, he's never let me see it.

He tips up my chin to study my face. His own is serious as he considers his words. My mate may be hotheaded and stubborn as a mule, but he's a leader for a reason and I'm, cautiously, learning to trust him. "Has this been bothering you, my mate?"

I shift uncomfortably. "Sort of...I mean, that's the whole reason you wanted to keep me. If I don't ever get pregnant, then all of this was for nothing."

My heart is in my throat as I study his face, but he merely smiles. "Mortania, there are other females who can produce young." His eyes turn predatory. If my whole body wasn't lax from the toxica it would have melted at his words. "If it worries you this much, we can always put more effort into breeding."

"More effort?" I screech. "You have me in the morning before rounds at the command center and at night before sleep. Sometimes you find me in the middle of the day! If we put more effort into it, we'd never leave the bed."

He takes my mouth for a searing kiss. "I'd be okay with that."

OUR MORNING ANTICS make Breccan late for his rounds, but he merely growls and stalks off, a pleased smile on his lips. A smile I put there.

I can only hope what I plan to do next won't steal that smile away for too long.

Once I settled into my life as a part of the faction, Hadrian and Oz had fought to give me tours to familiarize me with the layout of the facility. The cryochamber is down in the medical bay next to Avrell's office. I head there once Breccan is out of sight and hope no one stops me along the way.

Sayer, the linguistics expert, nods when I pass him near the nutrition bay, but he doesn't stop me. I say a quick prayer of thanks for his propensity to have his nose stuck in some book or another because he barely looks up as we cross paths. A sigh bursts from my lips and I press a hand to my churning stomach. Mouth bone dry, I gnaw at my lips and hope no one else is roaming the halls.

I'm not doing anything wrong. But it just *feels* wrong not to be completely honest with my guys. I've come to know and appreciate them and the last thing I want to do is betray them. But before I truly accept my fate here, I need to see the other women for myself and then talk to Breccan about what their plans are to wake them up. For most of my life, I've let things happen to me and those around me...not anymore. A weird twist of fate brought us here, and I'll be damned if I don't take care of the other girls.

Maybe it's all the talk of breeding and responsibilities. Maybe it's because I've spent so much time around the guys and long to see someone like me. I didn't realize how lonely it was to be the only human among a bunch of aliens. Whatever the reason, I reach the cryochamber and wave my armband under the scanner with my heart knocking against my ribs so violently, I fear I may pass out.

The screen beeps the familiar access tone and my bones turn to jelly in relief. I glance over my shoulder as I step through the door. The cameras will record my presence and by the time they question my visit, I'll have come up with an explanation. I don't think I'd get in trouble for being here, but I don't want an audience either.

It's not until I turn back around that I find I'm not alone in the room. The door closes too quickly behind me for me to slip back through, and then I'm trapped with a several cryotubes—the one I came from empty, the others still occupied—and a mort. I can't tell who.

I can't go back out without gaining his attention; it's a miracle he didn't notice me the first time. I hesitate for a few moments before I realize what he's doing. It takes a few minutes because the only light in the cryochamber is a faint blue color that emanates from the vertical tubes. The sleeping women don't require light, so most of the room is bathed in shadow.

At first, I think it's Avrell. He always seems to be running back and forth, checking their stats and testing them for genetic compatibility with the morts—something I've tried not to think about. I had a choice—if not at first, then certainly later—but these women don't. Maybe that's why I'm here. To give these women one.

I take a step closer and the mort shifts toward me.

Calix.

The blue glare from the tubes reflects on his glasses so I can't see his eyes. The stylus he carries religiously is tucked behind his pointed ear, forgotten. His claws are extended and scrape against the glass, the sound muted by the humming from the machines. Maybe that's why he didn't hear me enter. That, or he's so entranced with the woman in the tube in front of him that one of those geostorms could happen right now and he wouldn't notice.

My throat clamps closed, making speech impossible as Calix keys in a command on the tube's touchscreen that causes the window in front of the woman's body to slide open. He braces one arm on the cryotube over his head and lifts the other to press to the material of the thin gown she's wearing.

I try to rationalize what he's doing. He's the disease specialist. It makes sense that he'd be running tests on the women, but he doesn't have any equipment with him and the way he's touching her surely isn't clinical. The expression on his face is reverent, awed, but my brain skips right past that and to the violation that feels all too familiar.

"What are you doing?" I bark.

Calix blinks slowly, as if caught in a dream. "Aria?"

"Get your hands off of her."

He jerks them back and they tighten into fists by his side. "Does Breccan know you're here?"

"Oh, he will soon enough. What were you doing to her?"

"Doing?"

My stomach churns as Kevin's face swims in my vision. The image is fleeting, but it causes what little breakfast I've been able to eat to slosh uncomfortably. "Touching her like that."

"I wasn't hurting her." He looks appalled at the notion, but my anger isn't swayed.

"You shouldn't be touching her."

"She's to be my mate, Aria."

I press a hand to my belly and spin around, sure I'm going to be sick. "I've gotta go."

I don't even care if he sees the armband as I wave it in front of the sensor frantically. Calix follows close behind, but all I can think about is getting somewhere safe before I throw up all over the floor.

"Aria, wait!" he shouts behind me.

I can barely hear him over the ringing in my ears. He could catch me if he wanted, but he keeps a safe distance between himself and the crying female.

I run forever until I find Breccan near Galen's labs. He immediately smiles, but it turns into a frown as he rushes to my side. "What's wrong, my Aria?"

Calix hurries to us and Breccan growls. Calix immediately takes a cautious step backward. "I didn't harm her, before you tear out my throat."

"Then why does she look frightened?"

"I'm...not actually sure, Commander."

"Explain," Breccan orders me.

"I have your armband and went to see the women

in cryo." I say it all in one breath and don't give him a chance to react before I continue. "Calix was there and he was touching one of the women!"

He gives me a look that says we'll be talking about the armband later. To Calix, he says, "Is something wrong with one of the women?"

"No, Commander."

"You have to do something about this," I say.

"Mortania, I've known Calix my whole life. I trust him with it. I'm certain he didn't mean her any harm. You've come to know him as well, I'd hope. We want nothing more than to protect you."

I want to pull out my hair from the frustration. "We had a conversation about choices, Breccan! Doing anything to those women without their knowledge or consent is not okay."

He waves Calix away. "*We* also had a conversation about our people, Aria. If we don't impregnate them, and quickly, our men will soon die out."

"I thought I was okay with that, but I can't let you treat them like they aren't people. They're just like me."

"You are my mate and will be the mother of my young. You will listen to reason."

"I am your mate and the future mother of your child, but you don't own me! My thoughts are my own and you promised I'd be safe here, free to speak my own mind."

"You are in no danger. My men would die for you like they would for me. They've shown you again and again how they think of you as their own. Have I not proven my devotion to you?"

"Then *listen* to me. These women are people, just like me. They have feelings and hopes and dreams. Your men don't get to treat them as less than human. If you can't see that, then we have a problem here. I can't be with someone who would allow such a thing to happen. Don't you see?" A tear streaks down my cheek and I wipe it away. I hate crying. "Where do we draw the line? You may understand and respect me, but can you say the same for your men? What I saw Calix doing wasn't clinical or any part of his duties. It was predatory. I won't be a part of this cycle, not anymore."

"The aliens are my concern, Aria, as I am the commander of this facility. My men are only doing their part and carrying out my orders."

"But you're the high and mighty commander. If you intend for me to be a part of the faction, if you intend for *our child*, who is *half human*, to be a part of the faction, then the way you treat these women must change."

Breccan's ears flatten against his head and I

wonder if I've gone too far. How had we been so happy just a few short hours ago?

"Is that a threat?"

Another tear drops from my chin. I feel faint, but if this is the hill I choose to die on, I could choose worse. I remember how afraid I was when I woke up, alone, bleeding, and surrounded by strange aliens. As his mate, as a *commander's* mate, I can't help but feel like it's my job, my duty, to protect these women. I may not be able to send them home, but I can protect them here. At least to the best of my abilities.

My heart breaks at the fierce look on Breccan's face.

Even if it means losing the best thing that's ever happened to me.

[13]

BRECCAN

My ears flatten against my nog. I want to rage and destroy. Not because of Calix. Not because of Aria. Just the situation. Why does everything have to be so rekking complicated?

"A threat?" she hisses, her tears steadily streaming down her cheeks. My mouth waters to lick them away because they're so sweet but I know now's not the time. "If you don't care about my thoughts and feelings, then how can I care about *you*?"

I could choke Calix for causing my mate to become upset.

"Aria," I say, my tone softer. "You don't understand." She doesn't. She wasn't here when we watched our families die off one by one. She wasn't here when

we were terrified out of our minds. Successful reproduction with these aliens is so crucial. It's truly a
matter of life and death of an entire race.

"I think I have my answer," she utters out —then
hunches over and vomits without warning at her feet.

"Aria!" I bellow, and start for her as she becomes
wobbly and sways.

Thankfully, Calix is right behind her and catches
her before she collapses.

I quickly pull her into my arms and charge down
the corridor to Avrell's lab. His eyes are wide when I
burst in through the doors but he doesn't waste any
time and ushers me over to a bed. I lay her down and
she blinks slowly at me, her face pale. Snagging her
hand, I pepper kisses on the back of it.

"What's wrong with her?" I demand, my voice
harsh and violent.

He begins hooking her up to some machines, a
hopeful look on his face. His double fangs, while still
not as prominent as the others since he filed his down
some, show as he grins.

"Why are you so rekking happy?" I'm seconds
from climbing over the table and wiping the smile from
his face.

He picks up his wegloscan and waves it over her

abdomen. A flutter of hope dances inside my rib cage. It always lights up red. Red is the color of death and hopeless futures. Like the landscape of The Graveyard. Like the skies that are radioactive with harmful toxins. But the wegloscan isn't lighting up red.

It's green.

Like bitter green-bunches that we survive on when meat is nonexistent.

Like the color of the stones we collect from the underground wells that always sparkle with clean water coming from deep within the core of our planet, safe from the pathogens that plague everything else.

Green is life.

Green is a future.

I splay my palm over her flat stomach and grin at her. "Aria..." Then, I turn to Avrell. "Is it true?"

He's nodding, his eyes wide. "She is successfully impregnated."

I let out a loud chuckle of delight and look down at my sweet, fertile alien mate. But she isn't smiling. Her happiness has been swiped clean from her features and her brown eyes that always gleam with emotion are dead. Empty. Desolate.

"Aria," I mutter, worry causing my voice to become husky.

She sits up and shakes her nog at me when I reach for her. "Don't touch me."

A growl rumbles through me. I want to pull her into my arms and lick every part of her, worshipping her body like she is the sun. But then I remember her desires. This would further anger her and drive her away.

"Aria," I say again and hold up my palm, willing her to touch hers to mine. An apology. We'll work through this. She and the other aliens will carry our young. Our future isn't bleak anymore. It's shiny and brilliant.

She eyes my hand like I'm carrying The Rades. Her nostrils flared in disgust. Her lip curled up, baring her teeth at me. When I reach a little closer, she hisses like that of a young sabrevipe.

"Avrell," she instructs, her voice cold and hollow. "Show me to the navigation wing."

"The navigation wing has been closed for many revolutions," I snarl, my anger overtaking me. I boarded it up myself, unable to see more memories of our past for fear of succumbing to the depressing madness.

Color floods to her speckled cheeks and she points an accusatory finger my way. "It's the farthest location from you." Then she glowers at Calix. "And him. Send

Hadrian with me if you're worried about me being alone or if you want someone to watch over me."

"No," I snap. I want to yank her into my arms, and yet, I refrain. Every fiber of my being begs for me to do so. But my mate is fragile and angry. I won't undo everything we've worked so hard for. I won't betray my mate's trust, even when she is cross with me.

She closes her eyes for a moment, more hot tears leaking out. I want to lick them all away. Whisper promises to her.

"I'm moving out," she says firmly. "I need space from you. From all of you."

"Aria," I rumble out, my voice shaking. "You can't leave."

Her eyebrow shoots up, a challenging glimmer in her eyes. "I can. I will. You are going to let me."

Calix still won't look at me, his nog bowed in submission. Avrell remains still beside us. My hand fists and I drop it to my side, swallowing down the urge to stroke my claws through her soft hair.

"We should talk about this," I say, panic rising in my voice.

She gives me a clipped nod. "We will, eventually. But right now, I can't. I'm nauseated right now for many, many reasons. Avrell." She reaches over and grabs his elbow for support. His eyes dart to mine in confusion. I nod my command for him to escort her.

With a heavy, tearful sigh from my mate, they exit the lab.

My heart goes with them.

It's been three solars since Aria left. I'd thought she needed to let the anger simmer a bit but instead, she disappeared on me. When I returned to our chambers, her clothing and jewelry and favorite blanket were gone. She'd taken her goldenroot sweets too. Since she doesn't go far without those, I knew that she was serious at that point.

Each solar, long after the lights turn out, I toss and turn, inhaling her lingering scent that clings to my bedsheets. I'm losing my mind. The early solars, after we were forced into the facility, are forefront in my mind. The loneliness. The despair. The utter desperation for someone to swoop in and save us all.

No one came.

We slowly, solar by solar, had to climb our way out of the mental madness and cling to a hope that one solar we'd again be a flourishing and thriving people.

Little by little, we would make progress and do what we could.

There was always an inkling of hope that drove us along.

Now, I can't seem to latch on to this hope.

Desperate for something to take away the mental pain, I open the zuta-metal doors in the command center and let the UVs stream into the room. It takes strength but I refrain from unzipping my minnasuit and letting it scorch my flesh. But I don't need that anymore...not since her. What I need to do is think. I need to plan and make things better. Which is why I've called a meeting.

Everyone is here aside from Calix and Hadrian.

"Where's Calix?" I bark. I know where Hadrian is. He's taken to looking after my mate in my absence. As much as the beast inside me thrashes and screams in protest, I know it is for the best. He also keeps me apprised of her health and overall well-being. I'm grateful for his assistance. She trusts him and he is no threat to her.

Unlike me.

I close my eyes and push that thought out of my nog.

I would never threaten her. Her misinterpretation

is just that...a misinterpretation. When she has cooled, she will see. I will make her see.

"He's on his way. Said he had to stop by the lab to check on something," Sayer tells me, his eyes never leaving one of the old manuals that we've each read more times than I can count. His long black hair is twisted into the same sort of knot Aria wears sometimes on top of her nog. My heart clenches, knowing she taught him how to make the knot.

"Commander," Avrell says, his voice firm. "Close the zuta-metal doors."

I let out a groan but adhere to his command. The last thing I need is to be weakened by the UV rays. I need my mind sharp and my body strong. Once I've closed them, I stride over to the head of the table and take my seat. I glance around at the faction's morts, my most trusted men—my *only* men. Avrell is on my right, a tablet in his hand. His normally clipped hair is slightly disheveled and he appears to be fatigued. He's been working tirelessly each solar on the samples and the implantation attempts on the other aliens. I admire his devotion to the extension of our race.

Beside Avrell, Galen picks dirt from under his claw using a magknife. I try not to cringe. His shaggy hair hangs in his slanted eyes and his black brows are furled together. I know he spends each solar dedicating every ounce of energy to the seedlings he attempts to grow in his lab. If it weren't for his hard work, we'd have starved many revolutions ago.

"What's the status on the ship?" I ask, cracking the sub-bones in my neck. I'm tense. Completely.

Theron, who's been spinning all too quickly in his chair beside Galen, grabs the side of the table, his claws digging into the hard surface, and stops himself. "The ship has a name," he says dryly. "Sayer and I flushed the fuel capacitor on *Mayvina*. After our last run, we burned through our fuel and it's a rekking miracle we made it back home. Fumes, Commander. We made it back on fumes."

If I were one who prayed to the gods, I'd send up a thanks for allowing Aria to arrive in one piece.

"It's ready for another run?" I ask.

Theron shakes his nog and tugs a strip of fabric from his pocket and bites on it while he collects his shoulder-length black hair. Talking through his teeth, he says, "Not ready. While we were flushing the fuel capacitor, Sayer found a tear in the outer seam of the engine box." He ties the strip in his hair and shrugs. "That's Oz's specialty." He turns and motions at Oz, who sits beside him.

Oz smirks and pulls a greasy zuta-metal object from his pocket. "The tear in the outer seam was simple to fix. This?" He waves it in the air. "The deflection canister failed and who the rekk knows when. It's a wonder how the aliens didn't follow us right down to our planet and blow us all to The Eternals.

Theron snorts. "Because *Mayvina*," he enunciates, and gives me a pointed look, "purrs like a newborn sabrevipe and runs like an alpha rogstud." He shoots me a smug grin. "They can't ever keep up with the *Mayvina*. Even when my zuta-metal female is a bit ill and in need of repair. She never disappoints."

I refrain from rolling my eyes. "When will everything be operational on the *Mayvina*?"

"Soon," Theron assures me, his claws tapping on the table's surface. "Soon, Commander."

The seat opposite me on the far end of the large table that seats ten is empty. Draven leans up against the wall behind his seat, his eyes black and narrowed slits. Whereas the other morts' eyes only change when angry or extremely emotional, Draven's remain that way always. He assures me he is calm and of fit mind, but I see the madness that still lives within him. I'm not sure it will ever go away.

"What's the status on the beasts in the area? Have the geostorms driven the sabrevipes away?" I ask Draven. I'd love for them to get the rekk out of dodge so the rogcows will roam back our way. They're much finer eating.

He pulls away from the wall, eyes the open doorway, and then relaxes slightly. The self-inflicted scars along his bare arms are a constant reminder of the times he tried to scrape away the sores from his body when he was nearly dying from The Rades. They must bother him from time to time because unlike the rest of us, who wear full minnasuits that cover our arms, he's cut off the sleeves of all of his minnasuits. His black hair is clipped short and patchy in some places from the awkward regrowth after the disease. No one ever says anything about the scars or how The Rades ruined his body and mind.

"Sabrevipes are plentiful," he growls. "I did see some flying game just south a few mettalengths away from the facility."

I arch a brow at him. "From the tower?"

His eyes dart to the doorway again, always making sure there is an escape route. "The tower, Commander," he affirms, his voice unapologetic.

I clench my jaw and refrain from chiding him about spending so much time in the tower. The winds are brutal up there and you have to be completely covered from nog to toe in protective layers and a full mask. It's lonely, windy, and boring. I believe my lieutenant commander enjoys the openness. He suffers from the feeling of being trapped and the tower is yet another escape for him. Problem is, it's unsafe and open to predators. A sabrevipe can't climb that high but he's brought back the carcasses of venomous armworms that are known for nesting at those heights. Teeth incredibly sharp and they move quickly. Unlucky for them, Draven moves quicker.

"It's unsafe to travel that far from the facility," I remind him.

His black slit eyes bore into me. "Of course."

I'm unnerved by the glint in his gaze. Draven is a wild one. Sometimes I fear he'll simply disappear one solar. Just slip through the door and walk off into the great wide open.

Jareth, who sits across from Theron on the other side of Draven's empty chair, scribbles on a scrap of paper. His pale white hands are littered with tiny cuts and his short, pitch-black hair is sticking out in at least four different directions. He pushes the paper over to Sayer beside him, and Sayer nods, a smirk on his face. Sayer takes the paper and pushes it between the pages of his book and closes it.

"I need Calix's report," I grumble. "Where the rekk is he?"

Before anyone can answer, a loud, pained roar echoes from down the corridor.

I rise to my feet just as Calix tears into the command center with the force of a brutal geostorm. His black eyes are slits and his ears are flattened against his skull. He bares his teeth, his double fangs glinting in the light, and breathes heavily. In this moment, he is crazed. I worry he's contracted The Rades because the madness in his gaze matches that of Draven's.

"What is the matter?" I demand.

"I'm going to tear his mortarekking nog off his shoulders!" he bellows as he sends a chair flying into the wall.

By process of elimination, I say, "Hadrian?"

Calix glowers at me as Avrell rises beside me. Draven is tense across the room. Protocol states that if someone has symptoms of The Rades, you incapacitate and quarantine immediately.

He certainly doesn't look like his usual self. Gone are the glasses that belonged to Phalix—the only thing Calix recovered from father's decimated body. The stylus for his zenotablet that is always perched behind his ear is absent. His short, cropped hair is messy.

"Calix," Avrell says softly. "Let's get you down to

the lab so I can run some tests. You're not at all acting like—"

"They *took* her!" Calix roars, his sub-bones cracking and popping in his neck as he fully assumes his battle stance.

"Who took who?" I demand.

He hisses at me, his eyes wild with fury. "Hadrian and your *mate*. They took *my* lilapetal."

I blink at him in confusion and shoot Galen a troubled look. He's growing lilabushes and they're flowering at the moment. The pink, velvety flowers aren't edible, we've discovered, but he's found other uses for the petals that fall from the flowers. They're fragrant, and Galen has been making "soaps", as Aria calls it, with the petals.

"I don't understand," Galen says, holding up his palms.

"He's having hallucinations," Avrell grits out beside me. "I need him in the lab."

Calix shakes his nog and yanks at his hair. "No. No! You all rekking misunderstand." He shoots me a look of utter desperation. "They took *my* alien."

"*Your* alien?" I challenge.

He glowers at me. "When I touch her, her velvety skin turns pink. The alien's flesh reacts to my touch. She is meant to be my mate!"

"So, we're just walking in and claiming the ones we want?" Theron asks, a slight bite to his voice. "Had I known that was an option, I'd have claimed one the moment we landed the *Mayvina*."

"Calix!" I bellow. "Focus and tell me what happened." I shoot a hard glare Theron's way. "*Nobody* will be claiming *any* of the aliens."

Theron lets out a huff but backs down.

"I went to check on her. To lick away the tears that sometimes leak from her eyes. She likes when I straighten the unusual arm zuta-metal she wears." His eyes turn into round, black orbs and his ears release from his nog as he thinks of her. "She likes it when I rake my fingers through her locks of hair. The wrinkles that often form between her brows disappear. I know that in cryosleep they are supposed to be unaware, but with me, she responds physically to my touch and nearness."

He's infected all right.

But not by The Rades.

He's infected by the beautiful aliens who sing to our lonely hearts. Once they've gotten inside you, there is no getting them out. I think of my brave Aria. Standing up to the commander of the faction. Her body was weak and yet she was every bit as fierce as Draven.

And now, my mate has stolen one of the other aliens.

The alien, Calix's obsession, has been given a choice. Aria made that happen. Recklessly. She could put the alien at risk pulling her out of cryo without Avrell's help. Worry niggles at me but I have to trust in my mate's decision making.

I close my eyes...because the news I'm about to deliver won't sit well with any of them.

"Was the alien asleep or did my mate wake her?" I ask, needing to be sure.

Calix's black brows furrow together as he rambles out his explanation. "T-They woke her. Wrapped her in a blanket and walked her out of the cryochamber. I saw her between Aria and Hadrian as they took her to the navigation wing. I wanted to see what they were doing before I intervened, so I followed them to the wing. When I attempted to enter, Hadrian stood in the doorway and told me I was not to enter per Madam Commander's command." Calix's eyes narrow in anger. "Madam Commander? Since when?"

I rise to my full height and let the sub-bones in my neck crack loudly. My ears flatten against my skull as I growl. My battle stance is a fierce one, and the men under my command all lower their nogs in respect. Even desperate, lonely, sad Calix.

I hate this for them but there must be order, and if we are to have some sort of happiness in the long run, I'll need to establish some new rules until then.

"She is their leader. Aria Aloisius," I say, claiming her with my last name, "is Madam Commander of this faction and Alien Liaison. When it regards the aliens and their well-being, you seek council through myself or Madam Commander. This is the rule. A ceremony will soon make my words binding. Any mort disagree? I didn't think so."

Calix opens his mouth but I stop him with a wave of my hand. "Trust in Aria. She is wise and knows what is best for the aliens. They have different customs and needs than our race. I will meet with her to discuss the future of the others but at this time, she is in command of the newly awoken alien. I'll also advise her of the danger of waking them without Avrell's assistance. Make haste, Avrell," I tell him. "Please assist Aria and Hadrian with anything they should need." He rises and nods, his face paler than usual, no doubt worrying over the newly awoken one. I drag my gaze from his that probably matches my own and regard the other morts. "The navigation wing will become the female sub-faction. Morts aren't allowed to enter unless Madam Commander wills it."

Rekk.

Aria better know what she's doing.

My heart squeezes at the memory of her eyes lighting up with fierce fire as she bravely protected females she doesn't even know. Her dedication is admirable and her expertise is needed if we're going to make this work.

"This meeting is adjourned. Aria is hereby officially deemed Madam Commander and Alien Liaison."

They all nod.

Even Calix.

[14]
ARIA

FOR DAYS AND DAYS, I've hovered over the girl's bed, frowning like a mother over a newborn. My hand goes to my stomach as my thoughts flit to the life growing there. Everything has changed so much, so quickly, I haven't had time to think about what it'll mean when this one is born. I should be frightened. I've never given any thought to becoming a mother—not any real thought anyway. Most of my life has been spent surviving.

Now, I can't help but feel like I have two lives to fight for.

The girl shifts restlessly and I amend that thought. Now I have my child's life to protect, as well as the lives of all the females stranded on this lost planet.

Now, I admit to myself, it had been selfish, reckless

even, to move the girl so quickly. In my rash actions, I could have cost her life instead of saving it.

"She sure looks funny," Hadrian observes from his vantage point on the far side of the room. His words are hesitant, but he can't take his eyes off her.

"You don't need to stare, Hadrian," I bite out, then soften. "She needs rest."

But I fidget with the blanket. I'd been so sure of myself with Breccan at my side, so certain. He'd given me strength I'd never known I could possess.

Breccan, who'd come by each day since my departure to beg entrance, but I hadn't allowed Hadrian to let him past the door.

I glance back at the girl who hasn't woken up since we got her cleaned and changed three days ago. Her sunny yellow hair has turned limp and her pale skin has gone sickly white. I remember how ill I was after they woke me, but that was due to the miscarriage. My hand clutches the material of my dress at my stomach, my thoughts going back to my baby. The aliens had medicine, those bots, that could help her. It's selfish of me to keep potentially life-saving medicine for my own stubbornness.

I sigh. Breccan makes being a leader look so much easier than it is. This girl's life is in my hands. I can't let stubbornness, or pride, color my decisions like I had when I'd brought her here. If I am going to lead—alone or alongside Breccan—I have to start by realizing when I've made a mistake.

"We should have Avrell take another look at her," I say to Hadrian. Once they realized we not only woke her, but also took her, Avrell came to the rescue and he attached some machines to keep an eye on her.

"Do you think she's sick? Could she already be carrying a little mort?" I can't tell if he sounds hopeful or disappointed.

"I'm not sure. Maybe humans react to cryosleep differently. She doesn't look well," I admit reluctantly. "We should have taken her directly to the medical bay instead of bringing her here. That's my fault. I made a big deal about saving her and I won't let her die because of me." Avrell wasn't pleased at having to come to the sub-faction to look at her but he didn't argue. Simply did what he could and then left, but not before urging me to bring her in if things got worse.

"Do you want me to carry her there?"

I glance back at the girl's weak form. "I don't think we should move her right now. I'm worried it may be too much for her."

He stares at her a second longer, his face set, then turns to me and squeezes my shoulder "I'll hurry, Aria. We will fix her."

Smiling in gratitude, I say, "You're a good friend, Hadrian."

"A good *mate*," he corrects as he backs toward the door.

That makes my smile widen, even as it trembles with worry. "You'll make the best mate someday. Now go, hurry please."

I can do nothing else to help the sleeping girl, so I leave her in her quarters until Hadrian returns with Avrell. I have to keep busy, otherwise my mind races and I grow so depressed I don't want to get out of bed. But I can't languish the days away getting high and letting my life pass me by. I have people depending on me. Not only my baby, but this girl too, and all the women in cryo.

The morts have treated me well, that is undeniable. But they're still unused to humans and the women will need my help. The one not a few feet away needs me now. I *will* make up for what I've done, both to Breccan and to the new girl.

I head to the common room at the center of the navigation wing. It used to be what I assume was the main crew deck for the building before it came to be the facility. Since the morts' numbers are so small, they no longer need it. The large room serves my needs perfectly. With Hadrian's help, I've transformed it into a living room for when we wake the others.

Hadrian took furniture from the other living areas around the facility: a couple long, sleek, mod-looking couches and armless chairs. We arranged them around a low, thin coffee table with a large dish of goldenroot candies in the middle. He even fashioned a fireplace out of an old laser ray emitter to make the room feel homey. The effect works. Or, it would if I weren't so worried about the new girl and Breccan.

I pass through it now, on my way to the last of the living areas. There are six rooms, three on either side. One I've set up as a library of sorts. There are a ton of old manuals and a few history texts Hadrian managed to scavenge. I also stocked the shelves with blank tablets and paper, art supplies, and drawing implements for the future inhabitants. I hope it will be a soothing hobby for the women once they wake.

The other five rooms each contain small cots, a night table, a cabinet for clothes, and a small closet with a shower tube for cleaning. I still haven't gotten used to taking such intense showers that make you feel like a layer of your skin is missing afterward, frankly, but being clean is better than nothing.

I think Hadrian's enjoyed preparing the rooms for more people. He's mentioned on more than one occasion how happy he is to have more people joining the sub-faction.

Forcing myself to stop thinking, I go through each room, straightening things that don't need to be straightened and telling myself it will all work out. It has to.

The swoosh of the door alerts me to Hadrian's return. I make sure to move slowly out of one of the rooms. Going too quickly seems to trigger my upchuck reflexes. It doesn't take much these days, apparently.

"Did you get Avrell?" I ask as I move as quickly as my changing body will allow.

"I did," he answers hesitantly and steps out of the doorway to reveal not two, but three morts filling the entryway to the living quarters.

My eyes immediately narrow to Breccan's towering form. "What are you doing here?"

His expression is hard and unreadable, and I'd be lying if there wasn't a part of me concerned at his lack response. He's always looked at me with affection and desire, even in the beginning. I feel the loss of it like a punch. Not only had I risked the life of the girl I was trying to protect, but I'd alienated the only man who'd ever cared for me.

"I'm still the commander of this faction. All of its

members, including the alien ones, are my responsibility."

Hadrian steps in front of him and I hear his subbones crack menacingly. Breccan growls in return. A part of me softens even further at Hadrian's need to protect me. He's almost like the younger brother I never had.

"I don't want you to upset her," Hadrian says. "She's carrying the future for *all* morts, not just you."

Not wanting a fight and knowing it's important Avrell see the girl as soon as possible, I wave them into her room and give Hadrian a quelling look. "Now is not the time. This way," I add in Avrell's direction.

"Why haven't we done this with our living quarters?" I hear Avrell ask Breccan in a muted voice as they pass through the living areas.

"Hush," Breccan instructs, but when I peer back at them, I see his eyes roving appreciatively over my improvements. But none of the pretty decorations will mean anything if there is no one alive to appreciate them. I ignore him as his eyes land on me once he finishes his appraisal. I can't bear to see the disappointment from my reckless behavior.

The girl is awake for the first time since we brought her to the navigation wing. Her big blue eyes widen when the aliens come into the room. Her breathing quickens and I frown at the wheezing, rattling quality of it. Have her lungs been damaged by the cryotube?

Doubt burns at me relentlessly. Had I caused the damage?

"What's...going...on?" she asks around gasping breaths. Her wild eyes search the room, her breathing worsening as they land on Breccan, Avrell, and Hadrian.

Remembering the fear that had overtaken me after I woke up, I step forward in front of them, giving them a side eye to back off a little.

I take her hand in mine, careful of the monitors Avrell insisted she be hooked up to. Hearing her breathing now, I'm grateful he did. "Don't worry. I know everything feels scary and confusing right now, but we're here to help you. These are my friends. They won't hurt you."

"Where...am...I?"

"You're in a safe base on what I like to call The Lost Planet. My friend Avrell here is going to give you a scan—don't worry, it's painless—just to make sure you're healthy." Her breathing is still erratic, but her eyes aren't as wild as they were. "I'm Aria. What's your name?"

"E-Emery." She doesn't take her eyes off Avrell as

he steps forward with his portable scanner unit, but she also doesn't stop him as he examines her, even though her body trembles. From shock or fear, I'm not sure.

"You're safe here, Emery," I assure her. "I'm going to make sure of it."

Breccan rests a hand on my shoulder and I reach up automatically to take it. My heart twinges painfully in my chest when I realize what I'm doing, but I don't pull away for fear of further scaring Emery, who barely submits to Avrell's scanning. And if I'm being honest with myself, I've missed his hands on me. Missed his reassuring presence at my back, his kisses soothing away my pain. Truthfully, even though I doubt it's physiologically possible, I almost sense our child growing in my womb misses him, too.

Avrell concludes his scan and gestures for us to talk outside. My stomach revolts at the possibility that he may have bad news.

Emery makes a sound of surprise as we all start to file out, and I go to her side. "Don't worry. You're safe here in this facility. I know this is overwhelming, but please try to stay calm and rest. No one here is going to hurt you. I promise you that. I'll keep you safe."

"Who are all of you?" she asks, and relief floods through me at the even sound of her breathing.

"I'm Aria," I repeat. "The tallest one, Breccan," I gesture over my shoulder, "he's kind of like my husband. He's the commander of the...aliens here." I'm not sure how much information to give her. I don't want to scare her more than she already is, but I also don't want to keep her in the dark. One day at a time.

If possible, she blanches even more. "You're *married* to one of them?"

"Yes, sort of. There's a lot to explain, but we'll save that for later. I'll have one of them bring you something to eat and then you should rest for a while."

She takes my hand and I realize how much I've missed *human* touch. The morts have been welcoming, but I can't deny how good it feels to have someone like me here, too.

"I'm scared," she whispers.

"It's okay. I will protect you. Rest now."

She nods and is already dozing by the time I leave the room.

I find the three of them waiting for me in the living room, having made themselves quite at home on the cozy furniture.

Hadrian stands immediately at my entrance, a scowl on his face, but he keeps his mouth shut at a gesture from Breccan, who nods at Avrell.

Avrell merely sighs.

"How is she?" I ask him, ignoring the other two.

"Her O2 stats are a little concerning. I won't be certain of the cause without further testing, but there's no need for alarm until we have more data."

"So, she's going to be okay?"

He gives me a stern look and I bite my lip. "What you did was dangerous, Aria, but I don't believe it's the cause of her condition."

"Thank you," I say and leave it at that. I'm not going to argue with him about the severity of my actions. I have a feeling I'm going to get enough of a tongue lashing from Breccan.

"Stay with the alien," Breccan commands Hadrian. "Call for us if she wakes."

"Where are you going?" Hadrian asks, clearly torn over the man who raised him and his desire to help me. "I believe I should be near Madam Commander."

Breccan only seems mildly bothered by Hadrian's defiance. "You'll do as I say, Hadrian, or we'll have you for dinner instead of rogcow."

Hadrian shoots me a questioning look and I give him a nod. "It's okay. Give us some time to talk."

"I'll take the scan to my office to see if there are any other anomalies. When she's feeling up to it, though, she should come for a more extensive analysis." Looking uncomfortable, Avrell nods at no one in particular and then excuses himself. Hadrian reluctantly makes his way back over to Emery's room leaving me alone with Breccan for the first time in days.

The silence before he speaks threatens to overwhelm me, but there are no words left in me, no explanations. The truth was, I'd panicked and overreacted.

"Come with me," he finally says and holds out a hand.

I hesitate, but only to glance at Emery's room, where I can see her sleeping form, so still. "What about Emery?"

Was it just my imagination or was he trying to hide a smile?

"Hadrian will call for us if there is any change."

I place my hand in his and he tugs me from the navigation wing to an area of the facility I had only seen in passing. The chamber is full of suits and gear with a gigantic door that could only lead to the outside —a place I both fear and dream about. The freedom I'd coveted for so long now seems terrifying.

"Breccan, what are we doing here?"

He releases my hand to study the heavy duty suits hanging from the wall. After a few moments, he selects one and brings it to me. "Lift your leg," he instructs without answering my question.

I do as he says and he helps me into the suit, which fits a little loose, but doesn't fall off once he tightens all the straps. He dresses in his own and arranges helmets on our heads. A microphone screeches to life in my ear with a squeal.

"Uvie," Breccan says into it. "What are the R-levels today?"

"Plus point three, Commander," Uvie replies.

He finishes snapping us into our suits. "Prepare for an excursion."

"Where are we going?"

"I'm showing you my world, little alien. Now keep up with me, don't stray. If I tell you to do something, you do it right away. This world is dangerous, but I'll keep you safe."

He takes my hand as we leave through the doors and out into the brilliant outside world. A harsh wind kicks up dust and I'm thankful for the thick, tinted visor. Despite what looks like a dust storm, I hadn't realized how much I'd missed the open space. Breccan tugs me along a path carved into what looks like a mountain.

I don't speak, I can't, because I'm too busy taking in the sights around me. My senses are completely overwhelmed and the realization that I'm not home anymore hits me all over again.

I wonder if it will ever stop being a shock.

Up above the section of the mountain where the facility juts as proud and defiant as a mort brow ridge, Breccan pulls me to a stop at the peak. His voice is smooth as the finest liquor in my ear. I'm so distracted by how much I missed it, I don't even notice the words until he says, "Are you listening to me, mortania?

I glance up at him, the brilliant yellow haloing around his face and glinting off his protective gear. My stomach drops and tears prick at the back of my eyelids. They overflow and one drips down my cheek.

"I'm listening," I say, but my throat closes on the words.

"You're not listening, you're leaking, mortania," he says as he gestures to my tears. "Is your suit hurting you?"

Laughter mixes with tears. "No, I'm fine. Say it again?"

I hear his smile even over the communication device between our suits. "I knew you weren't listening." He tugs me in front of him so that I can see down the mountain and all the way across the horizon. The dust glitters in the whistling wind and sends sparks up into the golden light. I've never had much stock in magic, but he wraps his arms around me and I wonder to myself if it might be real.

The radio crackles and hisses, followed by his voice. "Do you want to go home?"

I want to turn to look at him, but he tightens his arms around my waist and he points to the highest point of the sky where the gold fades to white, then bursts into royal blue. Twin, pale ghosts of white float equidistant apart. If you squint, they appear to be two halves of a whole.

"Moons?" I ask in disbelief.

"The orbs, yes. I don't know of 'moons'. But beyond that is your world, yes? Your family. If this is what you want, what you're missing, I will find a way to give it to you."

This time I turn in his arms and he lets me. I search his eyes, but they're unreadable. He brushes a hand along the side of my mask and I yearn for his contact. "What-what are you saying?"

"You were so frightened of us—of Calix, who is one of the kindest of our faction—that you made a rash decision with the other little alien Emery. You were afraid of me."

The last bit he spits out like food that doesn't quite taste right. His words shame me and my gaze drops to the emblems in alien language I can't quite read.

"I've done my best to understand your ways. To make you as comfortable in our world as I can," he continues, then lifts my chin with a finger, "but if it's not enough, mortania, if you are still afraid, I won't keep you prisoner."

I pull out the first words my throat will allow me to say, "What about the other girls?"

"We'll figure out a way and they will all go home, if that's what you think is best."

The tears dry up and despite whatever mechanism there is in the suit that allows me to breathe, I'm having trouble drawing in oxygen. "But that would mean—that would mean your people...Breccan you wouldn't survive."

At this he brings my gaze back to his. "I want you to understand that your well-being means as much to me as my own morts. We're one now and your aliens are just as much a part of our faction as any other member. If going home is in their best interest, I will facilitate it."

"You can't do that." I think back to my conversation with Avrell. "Breccan you'd die. You'd all die." I press a hand to my stomach. What would happen to our child?

"I used to think so," he admits. "But you taught me different."

"Me?" I say incredulously.

"Who else? You taught me strength when I

thought I had none left. You taught me to care again when I wanted nothing more than to let myself burn up with this planet. For that I owe you the world. I owe you whatever life you want for yourself, for those aliens in cryo."

"I don't know what to say," I tell him. "After the way I treated you, the things I did, why would you even want me to stay?"

"I'll always want you, Aria. Always. I want you to be my mate, my wife as you say. I want you to take my name in truth and lead by my side—for both morts and aliens. But only if that's what you want as well."

I don't have to think about it. My throat closes and I choke out, "Breccan. I want you. I want us."

He rests his mask against mine, his eyes glued to mine. His forked tongue flicks out like he wants to lick away the salt of my tears if the masks weren't in the way. "You are more important than my own life. Than anything. No solar is worth living without you in it. You are more addicting than any sun, and without you, my world is dark. Come on. We've been out here far too long."

We walk back inside where he takes me through a rigorous cleansing in the decontamination bay. It's a reminder of how toxic their world is out there and how safe it is inside. Once we're clean and our zu-gear has long been removed, he pins me against a wall, his strong hips against mine. His fingers twist in my hair as he regards me with a pained expression.

"Please come back to me, my Aria," he murmurs, "and light up my life again."

[15]
BRECCAN

BACK IN THE FACILITY, her scent overwhelms me. Heady and seductive. She practically drips with something I am desperate to taste. Avrell explained to me that the female hormones and secretions were more potent once successful implantation has occurred. He told me that it's supposed to increase each solar as she grows to accommodate our mortling. If she smells this good already, I can't even begin to imagine how she'll smell many solars from now.

"Breccan," Aria murmurs, her nose turning pink. "I'm nervous."

Now that she's in my grip again, I'm afraid to let her go. I want to clutch on to her forever. And I *will* hold her until she pushes me away. I'll always hold her. "Why, mortania?"

She smiles, not wide enough to show her useless teeth, but enough to let me know she's missed my compliments. "What if I'm not a good mom to our baby? I made so many mistakes. I don't want to make anymore."

I furrow my brows as I pluck words out and try to place the meanings—words she's used in the past. Mom means mother. Baby means mortling. "You will be the best mother. Look how fiercely protective you are over the awoken one."

I'm worried about the awoken one because there are nine other morts who'd love to have their chance at claiming a mate. I am not sure how long I can keep them in line before their baser instincts take over. Mine certainly did with Aria, and once that happens, there's no stopping it. Consequences mean nothing when the possibility of having a mate filling your lonely world is within reach.

Her shoulders, which were slouched forward, go back and she bravely lifts her chin, revealing to me her strength. The alien females don't have sub-bones or ears that move. They don't even growl. Their signs of strength are different. A raising of the chin. A flaming in their eyes. A flare of their nostrils. My alien is always displaying how brave and strong she is. This is exactly why she is best suited for the position I have created for her.

"We will have a ceremony. One where you will be officially named Madam Commander and Alien Liaison."

She wraps her arms around my body and presses her breasts against my chest. Her body heat penetrates through our minnasuits. The suit Calix designed for her speaks to carnal parts of me. I want to puncture the material with my claw and tear through it until her swollen breasts have escaped their captivity.

"Breccan," Aria says sharply. "You're growling."

I blink away my daze. "You just..."

"Smell freaking amazing?" she offers, her lips quirking up on one side.

"Precisely. Avrell explained that during implantation, your scent would become..."

"How does that explain *you* smelling better, then?" she asks in confusion.

"I don't know, but I need you to come back home. With me. Please, Aria." I cradle her delicate face with my massive hands. She's so tiny and fragile, yet she is unbreakable. It's a madness for my mind to compute. A paradox. "I need my mate." In ways that I can't explain right now.

She gives me a slight nod and before she can suck in her next breath, I have her scooped in my arms as I stride from the sub-faction. She struggles from my grasp as we pass the other female's quarters. Not wanting to harm her or our mortling, I release her to her feet.

"What is it?"

"I promised Emery I wouldn't leave her alone." She glances over her shoulder at the door. "Give me a second to check on her. I don't want to abandon her on her first few days. I've already messed up so many things, I don't want to break my promise, too."

As much as I want to drag her back into my arms, pride glows in my chest. Pride for my mate. I nod to her and she flashes a brilliant smile. My mate is pleased.

She turns and enters the room with me close behind. As I go to enter, she waves a hand and widens her eyes, motioning for me to stay. I bare my teeth at her in jest, but stay out of sight of the other alien.

"How is she?" I hear her ask Avrell, who has been by each day to run his tests and take his samples.

"Her breathing is still labored, but she's in good spirits," Avrell replies. "She's resting now as I gave her a dose of the microbots in an attempt to heal whatever ails her lungs."

"How long will it take?" Aria asks.

"We'll know soon if they are effective, but she's been weak so she may rest for some time yet."

At that, I peer around the corner and catch Aria's eyes with mine. Her cheeks flush with color.

"Will you call if there are any changes?" she asks. Her feet inch toward me and my cock hardens. *So close.*

"Of course," he says. I ignore the playful humor in his voice.

She speeds into my arms like a shot from a zonnoblaster and I lift her and turn. The doors all flash by as I practically run toward our chambers.

Our chambers. She may have moved her things but she never left, for she lives inside my heart. Always there with me no matter what. When I carry her over the threshold, she lets out a giggle.

"Where I come from, when the husband carries his wife into their home, they are officially married and ready to start their life," she says, her fingers stroking through my long black hair.

"We are officially everything," I tell her. "And we've already started. Here, we belong to each other the moment we mutually claim it as so. You've been mine for a while now, Aria."

She grins at me as I set her on her feet. With sure movements, she unfastens her suit. The moment her breasts are free, she lets out a sigh of relief. I think we need to work on some new clothes. Those are a snug fit and with all the growing I'll soon do, I'll need something I can breathe in."

I peel away my own minnasuit, my eyes never leaving her naked flesh. I cannot see any swells indicating my *baby*, but Avrell assures me it lives inside of her. I'm eager to watch her grow as her body accommodates the mortling.

"You're growling again," she says, her brown eyes darkening with hunger.

"I see something I would love to taste," I rumble. My cock is hard and aching. As I step forward, toward my mate, my heavy erection bobs with my movement.

Her eyes travel down and then she bites on her bottom lip. Someone else is hungry too, it would seem.

"I want to lick inside every part of your mouth," I murmur.

She snorts. "That shouldn't sound so romantic but I know what your licking leads to..." Her gaze finds mine and fire blazes within it.

My hands find her hips and I haul her to me. A twitch of my cock between us alerts her to my eagerness to mate.

"Make love to me," she murmurs, her fingers

sliding up my chest. She stands on her toes and offers her sweet mouth to me.

I tangle my clawed fingers in her glossy hair and angle her nog so that I may have the best access to her pouty lips. She parts her pink, plump lips. Another growl escapes me as my mouth captures hers. The moment my forked tongue dives into her, I'm blissed out. She intoxicates me like the UV rays I'd become addicted to but she doesn't harm me. No, my little alien nourishes me. She fills voids that were hollow for so long. She brings life to parts I had long thought dead.

My tongue slides along her dulled teeth and dances with her short stubby tongue. Her eagerness matches my own. Each of us so desperately needs the other. Between us, my cock seeps at the crown, my seed useless now that she is with child. But I still crave to fill her up with it. I love watching the milky essence leak out of her red, swollen cunt after we've mated. It's fascinating and fulfilling.

"I need you right now, Brec," she whimpers. "Right now."

I grab a handful of her round rump with one hand and lift her. She wraps her legs around my waist as she all but climbs me. Her fingers latch around the back of my neck, her lips never breaking from mine. With my free hand, I rub the crown of my dripping cock against her soaked center. She cries out, the sound unlike any I've ever heard. So filled with need and longing.

I walk with her to the nearest wall and press her back against it. Slowly, I push into her tight heat, relishing the way she throws her nog back, breaks our kiss, and bellows my name. With a growl, I slam into her. Pleasure explodes around me. Having her seated on my cock is the best feeling in this dead and broken world. She brings life to this planet. She brings life to me.

A sharp metallic scent fills the air, and it's then I realize my claws have punctured her fleshy bottom. Panic ripples through me but she finds her orgasm with an intense shudder. Her cunt grips my cock so hard, I forget about everything aside from claiming my female. My seed spills from me, hot and violent, as I thrust wildly into her. I can sense the toxica rendering her useless because she relaxes completely in my arms.

"Brecccaaannnn," she whispers, drawing out my name.

"I have you, little alien. You're protected. I will not hurt you." I cringe knowing I've drawn her blood, but I don't speak of these things since she seems satisfied.

Carrying her over to our bed, I make sure to lick and suck on her tongue along the way. She lets out a pleased groan when I sit on the bed and then pull her against me as I lie down. I've learned she prefers to be the one on top after our *lovemaking* moments, as she calls them.

"My heart aches for you nonstop, mortania," I tell her, my voice low and full of emotion for this female. "Nonstop."

A tear leaks from the corner of her eyes and I crave to lick it. Perhaps later.

"Love," she croaks.

I stroke her hair. "Love?"

"That is love," she murmurs. I can feel her tiny palm that's splayed on my chest begin to lift.

"This is love," I agree, sliding my hand beneath hers.

She curls her dainty fingers between mine and sighs. "Mine. You're mine."

I inhale her scent, which is no longer so potent, and I wonder if it has something to do with the fact that we've finally given in to what we've been fighting the past few solars. "Yours," I agree. "You're mine too."

"Always."

I STAND at the podium with Draven to my left and Aria to my right. As lieutenant commander, it's Draven's duty to assist in the ceremonies when we promote our morts to positions they are best suited for. This is something that didn't come from any manuals that existed before us or stories passed down from our parents. This is something I created to improve morale among my morts. It gives them a sense of purpose and pride. In our decimated world, we need all the help we can get, finding something to look forward to each solar.

Scanning the command center, I'm pleased to see the members of our faction dressed in their fanciest attire. Minnasuits adorned with precious stones pulled from the depths of the underground wells, and zuta-metals stamped and molded by Oz. Beautiful, shiny pieces sewn onto the suits to make them more attractive. The only one we're missing is Hadrian, and another thump of pride thunders in my chest. He is no longer an apprentice. For now, he will serve as Madam Commander's Hand. His strength and knowledge of this world will be useful to her as she makes decisions regarding her people. It is a great honor for him, and soon we will have a ceremony naming him as well.

Calix is broody this solar but he sits up straight and alert. He is the most immaculate, of course, with not a stray fiber on his clothing. His zuta-metals are the shiniest and I know his rocks are the cleanest. I'm glad to see him more like his usual self. For a few solars, I'd been worried we'd have to lock him up in a reform cell until he could get a handle on his abrupt insanity over the awoken one.

Quickly, I scan my morts, giving them all nods of respect, ending with Draven. Then, I flash Aria an encouraging smile and try not to let my gaze linger too long on her swollen breasts that nearly spill from the top of her suit.

"Our planet, Mortuus, is lost and dying. A desolate place where a few lone survivors dwell. We had lost hope. Our future was bleak. Longevity was a luxury we couldn't afford. The most we could hope for was survival. We'd all but given up," I say, my voice hoarse and husky.

I reach for Aria's hand and she gifts it to me, her fingers linking with mine in a display of unity. "But our future has been restored. A seed planted and hope delivered to us like a savory treat. We are no longer lonely. We are no longer without prospect. Aria Aloisius, my mate and wife, has come to us bearing contributions to our world that only she and her people can offer. It will not come without struggle. It will not come without consequence. But, together," I squeeze her hand, "together, we can once again grow and inhabit this lonely planet. We can rebuild our people and have families."

I face my men and crack the sub-bones in my neck. My ears flatten and a growl rumbles through me. They all bow their nogs in submission, including my sweet alien. It prides me to know they trust in my leadership. I will never let them down.

"I am Breccan Aloisius, the forgotten commander. My people will have the future they deserve. I'll make sure of it. But it will not be at the expense of the aliens. With Aria Aloisius's help, we will create an atmosphere where morts and the aliens can coexist. Reproduction and societal growth will always be of extreme importance. However, it won't rank over true relationships. The aliens are to be respected, and all morts will honor Madam Commander's laws regarding the females. When it comes to breeding, it will be by their choice and timeline. They'll be educated on the importance, but never coerced. All implantation of aliens in cryosleep will cease, for they cannot make their own decisions in that state. They will not be forced into anything they do not want to do, for we are not Kevins."

While the other morts exchange confused glances, Aria lets out a small snort. "No, you're not."

"On this solar, let it be known that Aria Aloisius is hereby deemed Madam Commander and Alien Liaison. Where it regards the aliens, she makes all decisions. I will be her council and together we'll make this work. All those in favor," I bark, my eyes darting to each one.

"Aye," they all bark back at once, a unified front.

"All those not in favor?" I ask. The silence warms me. "Very well."

Draven's deep, rumbly voice delivers the final decree. "Our faction of this facility, the only living morts on Mortuus, deem Aria Aloisius as Madam Commander and Alien Liaison. It is done."

And it is.

As everyone begins to stand, the ceremony over, Aria holds up a hand.

"Please," she says firmly. "Stay seated for a moment." Her eyes dart my way and happiness dances in her brown-eyed gaze. "We humans have our own ceremony. Between two married people. Oz?"

Oz, grinning like a rogstud eager to rut, stands and pulls something from the pocket of his minnasuit. He hands it to Aria.

"Thank you." She nods, dismissing him. Once he's seated, she turns to me. "Breccan, when I woke up that day, I was terrified. All these big scary guys staring at me as if I were their only hope. Not only was it intimidating, it was overwhelming. The responsibility that came with your hope was so intense. Me, one woman, was to help pave a way for your people. I was frightened and unsure, but as time passed and I fell in love with you, life began to feel right here.

"My life back home was horrible. Looking back, I didn't realize how I, too, was living without hope. Existing without truly feeling. It wasn't until I was thrown into your care that I began to search out who I really am. I can't thank you and the others enough for allowing me to find the real Aria. I have purpose now. As your partner and leader of the human females."

I bow my nog to her. "You are most welcome, mortania."

She smiles as she takes one of my fingers and slides on a zuta-metal band. It has etchings and catches the light. "Oh, thank God, it fits."

Frowning, I inspect the zuta-metal on my finger. It fits comfortably but I wonder its purpose. She hands me a smaller zuta-metal band that has a shiny stone wedged between four prongs. It glitters in my palm.

"Put it on my same finger," she instructs.

Carefully, so as not to snag her delicate flesh with my claws, I slide the small band onto her finger.

"Wedding rings," she informs me. "It binds our

promises to each other. It's a human thing." She winks at me. "Now, Commander, you may kiss your bride." Her brown eyes are liquid fire as she parts her lips, just begging to be tasted.

I haul her to me, loving the squeal from her and the way her breasts smash against me, and devour her sweet mouth. I lick and taste her long after everyone leaves the room. And when it's empty, I peel away her clothes and taste her some more. Everywhere.

From my vantage point, I can see straight into the sub-faction. She—Emery, as they say—is so fragile. Like the fine petals of a lilabush. But unlike the healthy flowers that grow in Galen's lab, this one wilts. With each passing solar, her skin grows more pallid. The tiny coughs rattle from her chest and her breaths come out labored.

Aria has been distracted creating the home for the humans and readying the space for the others to be woken up, but she is overlooking the needs of my lilapetal. She is letting her die before our very eyes.

As usual, when I'm stealing gazes of Emery, her nog will slowly turn and seek me out. She does not smile for she is too weak. She does not gesture in greeting. All she does is cry. Silently. Motionless. The tears

I've tasted while she was in cryosleep were unlike anything my forked tongue has ever had the pleasure of licking. I crave to hold her in my solid arms and lick away her sweet sadness.

But I am not allowed to hold her.

Aria demands that I keep my distance until Emery can decide these things for herself. They do not understand that I've studied her expressions long before she became the next awoken one. I feel attuned to her. She coughs and sputters, and yet I do not fear the pathogens that litter the air around her. It is unimportant to me because her well-being trumps all. The idea of anyone else coughing like that is enough to have me running back to the lab and sitting under the equalizer to eliminate the bacteria.

Emery, I'd gladly catch whatever it is she ails from.

Then I could hold her while it stole us both from this life.

Nobody, especially Emery, deserves to die alone.

I won't rekking allow it.

With my eyes locked on hers, I try to read her expressions. She's sad but mostly worried. Using what little energy she does have, she tugs and twists at the zuta-metal that is around her arm. I feel like it unlocks an important secret about her. I've scoured through the test results Avrell has obtained from her and read through his notes.

For someone so brilliant, our faction's physician is plagued with not knowing what to do.

There's a name for her ailment. She spoke it to Aria and it's been recorded, but it means nothing to us morts. Asthma. Inhaler. All we know is her lungs struggle even on her own planet, but at least there she had the proper medicine. She is too weak for us to try to send her back. It's been discussed. With space's compression on one's lungs, she would not survive. That is written in Avrell's notes as well.

Which means...

There is only one thing left to do.

I study contagious diseases and pathogens. I find cures for our people. It's what I'm good at. Like second nature. This will be no different. I won't stop until I've done it.

Quietly, I step into the sub-faction and stalk her way, thankful that Hadrian is nowhere to be seen. Her eyes widen in surprise but she does not call out. Something that resembles relief flashes in her bright blue eyes. It's enough to fuel me forward on my mission—a mission that'll no doubt get me locked away in a reform cell, should Breccan and the others intercept it.

I cannot fail.

Kneeling beside her, I hover my palm over her cheek, desperate to touch her. But Aria's commanding words still ring in my nog. Her laws about only touching if they ask. Hesitation swirls inside of me like the stirrings of an epic geostorm.

"Help me," Emery croaks out, her body shuddering slightly as she pleads. "Help me or I will die."

I allow my palm to stroke the side of her face—and then I do the unthinkable.

I gently pull my fading alien into my arms, careful not to break her, and carry her out of her home.

With haste, I rush back to my lab, where I will lock us away. They'll find us eventually, but I will have to make sure they can't get in. I'll work relentlessly, undisturbed by them, until I find a cure.

I *will* rekking save her.

"Relax now, lilapetal," I urge, my voice soft, just for her. "I'm going to heal you."

Or I'll die trying.

Keep reading with the next installment...
THE VANISHED SPECIALIST!

ACKNOWLEDGMENTS

K WEBSTER

Thank you to my husband. You're my biggest supporter and my inspiration. I love you to the moon and back, my fellow weirdo.

A big giant thank you to Nicole Blanchard for loving aliens and all things strange every bit as much as I do. Our mutual obsession is what brought this awesome book to fruition. So many nerdy talks over many nights as we built OUR WORLD. I can't think of anyone I'd rather do this with than you! You rock, lady!

A huge thank you to my Krazy for K Webster's Books reader group. You all are insanely supportive and I can't thank you enough. I love when y'all get

Krazy with me and read things you wouldn't normally read because you're curious like me!

A gigantic thank you to those who helped me with this book. Elizabeth Clinton, Ella Stewart, Misty Walker, Holly Sparks, Jillian Ruize, and Gina Behrends—you ladies are my rock!

A big thank you to my author friends who have given me your friendship and your support. You have no idea how much that means to me.

Thank you to all of my blogger friends both big and small that go above and beyond to always share my stuff. You all rock! #AllBlogsMatter

Kelli Collins, thank you SO much for editing this book. You're a rock star and I can't thank you enough! Love you!

A big thanks to IndieSage PR for pimping us out!

Lastly but certainly not least of all, thank you to all of the wonderful readers out there who are willing to hear my story and enjoy my characters like I do. It means the world to me!

NICOLE BLANCHARD

This year has been a hard one for me, but this book, these characters, this series, and my co-author have given me something to look forward to each day. A place to escape to. I hope the same proves true for you.

I'd like to thank K, first and foremost, for digging aliens as much as I do. Thank you for pushing me, supporting me, and being my idol. You are an amazing person and I'm beyond grateful to call you my friend. Here's to many, many more dirty alien books together.

My Knockouts. I wouldn't be here if it weren't for you. So many of you have been rooting for me since the beginning and I can't tell you how thankful I am to have you by my side. You chicks are AMAZING!

Melissa. Melissa. Melissa. I thank you every book and I will continue to do so because you quite simply are amazing. You fork me good!

Thank you to my beta readers: Amber Lynn, Cindy Camp, and Debbie Adams-Rice.

A big thank you to Alana Albertson, my twin. It's been a rollercoaster half a decade together, but you've been there every step of the way. My eternal gratitude for always having my back.

To our team, Kelli Collins and the IndieSage PR bloggers. We couldn't have done this without you!

Readers along with me on this journey. Thank you for taking a chance on me. I hope we can continue share many wild stories together!

K Webster is a *USA Today Best-selling author*. Her titles have claimed many bestseller tags in numerous categories, are translated in multiple languages, and have been adapted into audiobooks. She lives in "Tornado Alley" with her husband, two children, and her baby dog named Blue. When she's not writing, she's reading, drinking copious amounts of coffee, and researching aliens.

facebook.com/authorkwebster

twitter.com/KristiWebster

instagram.com/authorkwebster

amazon.com/K-Webster

bookbub.com/authors/k-webster

goodreads.com/K_Webster

Psychological Romance Standalones:

My Torin

Whispers and the Roars

Cold Cole Heart

Blue Hill Blood

Romantic Suspense Standalones:

Dirty Ugly Toy

El Malo

Notice

Sweet Jayne

The Road Back to Us

Surviving Harley

Love and Law

Moth to a Flame

Erased

Extremely Forbidden Romance Standalones:

The Wild

Hale

Like Dragonflies

Taboo Treats:

Bad Bad Bad

Coach Long

Ex-Rated Attraction

Mr. Blakely

Easton

Crybaby

Lawn Boys

Malfeasance

Renner's Rules

The Glue

Dane

Enzo

Red Hot Winter

Dr. Dan

KKinky Reads Collection:

Share Me

Choke Me

Daddy Me

Watch Me

Hurt Me

Contemporary Romance Standalones:

Wicked Lies Boys Tell

The Day She Cried

Untimely You

Heath

Sundays are for Hangovers

A Merry Christmas with Judy

Zeke's Eden

Schooled by a Senior

Give Me Yesterday

Sunshine and the Stalker

Bidding for Keeps

B-Sides and Rarities

Paranormal Romance Standalones:

Apartment 2B

Running Free

Mad Sea

2 Lovers Series:

Text 2 Lovers (Book 1)

Hate 2 Lovers (Book 2)

Thieves 2 Lovers (Book 3)

Pretty Little Dolls Series:

Pretty Stolen Dolls (Book 1)

Pretty Lost Dolls (Book 2)

Pretty New Doll (Book 3)

Pretty Broken Dolls (Book 4)

The V Games Series:

Vlad (Book 1)

Ven (Book 2)

Vas (Book 3)

Four Fathers Books:

Pearson

Four Sons Books:

Camden

Elite Seven Books:

Gluttony

Greed

Not Safe for Amazon Books:

The Wild

Hale

Bad Bad Bad

This is War, Baby

Like Dragonflies

The Breaking the Rules Series:

Broken (Book 1)

Wrong (Book 2)

Scarred (Book 3)

Mistake (Book 4)

Crushed (Book 5 – a novella)

The Vegas Aces Series:

Rock Country (Book 1)

Rock Heart (Book 2)

Rock Bottom (Book 3)

The Becoming Her Series:

Becoming Lady Thomas (Book 1)

Becoming Countess Dumont (Book 2)

Becoming Mrs. Benedict (Book 3)

Alpha & Omega Duet:

Alpha & Omega (Book 1)

Omega & Love (Book 2)

Nicole Blanchard is the *New York Times* and *USA Today* best-selling author of gritty romantic suspense and heartwarming new adult romance. She and her family reside in the south along with their menagerie of pets. Visit her website www.authornicoleblanchard.com for more information or to subscribe to her newsletter for updates on sales and new releases. P.S. there's also a free book!

facebook.com/authornicoleblanchard

twitter.com/blanchardbooks

instagram.com/authornicoleblanchard

amazon.com/Nicole-Blanchard

bookbub.com/authors/nicole-blanchard

goodreads.com/nicole_blanchard

Friend Zone

Frenemies

Friends with Benefits

Box Set

The Lost Planet Series

The Forgotten Commander

The Vanished Specialist

The Mad Lieutenant

Journey to the Lost Planet (Books 1-3)

The Uncertain Scientist

The Lonely Orphan

The Rogue Captain

Return to the Lost Planet (Books 4-6)

The Determined Hero

The Arrogant Genius

The Runaway Alien

Saving the Lost Planet (Books 7-9)

Dark Romance

Toxic

An Immortal Fairy Tale Series

Deal with the Dragon

Vow to the Vampire

Kiss from the King

Standalone Novellas

Bear with Me

Darkest Desires

Mechanical Hearts